THE KEEPERS

By Sherry Valdez

Dedicated to Lynn Franklin

Friend and mentor

Contents

ONE

Blackberry Lane

When I was five years old, I assumed all children fell asleep the same way I did; in a moonlit room, with a million crickets chirping outside the window. I dreaded bedtime, mostly because it was never my idea. Each night I fought the same battle, trying to shut off thought and imagination long enough to fall asleep. I tossed and turned and constantly flipped my pillow, with hopes that one side would feel cooler than the other.

High humidity and the absence of air conditioning made for a long summer's night. And it never failed that when I finally nodded off, the buzz of a lone mosquito roused me wide-eyed and alert. I slapped blindly into the darkness, which rarely rid me of the pesky insect. I usually resorted to hiding from it, and pulled the crisp cotton sheet over my head. But the thick Oklahoma air made it too unbearable. Covers cast aside, I rolled over to face the screened window. Eventually, a southern breeze was sure to blow in, part the pink curtains, and cool down my damp cheeks.

Before long, the song of the fields began. Out in the darkness, night creatures came to life; whip-poor-wills called, katydids whirred, and bullfrogs croaked. Comforted by their chorus, I drifted off and slept soundly for the rest of the night.

The year was 1962, and I was finally old enough to spend weekends with Grandma Janie. My Granddad, Jakob Samuels, had passed away one year ago, so it was my responsibility to keep her company, or so I believed. My two cousins, Gunner and Mitch, felt the same way. Being the only girl, as well as the youngest grandchild, I loved the moments when I had my grandmother's undivided attention. But I also had fierce competition, as the boys simply wouldn't allow it to go on for very for long. Grandma Janie often reminded me that their love for her was just as great as my own.

Grandma's farm was sometimes the center of activity in our small, unincorporated community of Waya, which means "wolf" in the Cherokee language. She'd lived here for over sixty years, and most everyone knew her and treated her like family. Whether kin or not, she was referred to as "Grandma Samuels," a role she accepted with great pride. Grandma was always available with a word of wisdom, or a shoulder to cry on; and it was quite common to find her with visitors. Her comfortable, single-story home was tidy and welcoming. And if things became too quiet, that was a sure sign the black wall phone would soon ring. There was always a pitcher of sweet tea in the fridge, and something savory simmering on the cook stove.

Jane Elizabeth Red Eagle Samuels—Grandma—was born here on her property in 1901, when Oklahoma was still known as Indian Territory. Her parents Elias and Brannagh Red Eagle, received the twenty-acre farm as a wedding gift. They'd added acreage by buying out neighbors who came and went over the years. Eventually, the farm grew to one hundred acres. The land, rich and high-yielding, ensured a comfortable living for their family.

Grandma's parents had unique heritages. Elias's Cherokee family arrived at Indian Territory via the Trail of Tears. After the discovery of gold in their home state of Georgia, the Indian Removal Act of 1830 pushed out the tribes who lived there, and allocated them to unsettled land west of the Mississippi River. Though some tribes moved on without incident, others protested and refused. Brutal force was often used by the government. Helpless and vulnerable, Native Americans were rounded up by federal troops and herded like cattle. Thousands of men, women, and children were torn from their ancestral lands and forced to make the harrowing journey across several states to Indian Territory. Many died of disease, malnutrition, or exposure along the way. The trip, which was mostly on foot, ended in Tahlequah, which sits at the base of the Ozark Mountain range. Cherokee survivors remembered their journey as *nu na da ul tsun yi,* meaning "the place where they cried."

As a boy, Elias was required to assist his father with harvest. Their wheat crops were taken by horse and wagon teams, and delivered to a nearby millhouse, owned by a "Black Irish" immigrant named Tomas Dempsey. Once the wheat was received at the millhouse, it went into a hopper and through a large grinder, and then processed into flour.

The millhouse was also the place where Elias first laid eyes upon Brannagh Dempsey, the owner's daughter. From that moment on, he eagerly volunteered to skip school during harvest, just to get a mere glimpse of her. Elias was twelve years old at the time, and she seemed to be close to his own age. Brannagh's appearance called to mind a porcelain doll, with her light complexion and raven hair. It took a couple of years before he finally worked up the nerve to approach her. As she left Stanton's General Store one day, he seized the opportunity.

Brannagh, with a stack of school books in her arms, jumped from a steep wooden walkway. Her feet slipped in the mud, and she lost her balance. Like Johnny-on-the-spot, Elias reached to steady her. Their eyes met, and he gave her a quick nod. She whirled to study him, then thanked him and rushed away. The brief encounter made Elias' day. With harvest ending and winter on its way, he knew that if he wanted to get acquainted with her, he'd best act fast.

A week later, while in town with a neighbor, Elias looked everywhere for Brannagh, but to no avail. When it was time to make the journey back home, Elias settled onto the wagon seat, and took a final look around. What happened next would become forever etched in his memory. Brannagh exited the millhouse office, a sight to behold; she wore a dress of emerald green with a matching bow in her dark curls. She noticed him and stopped in her tracks. Elias swallowed hard and sat up straight. He lifted his hand to wave, and to his surprise, she smiled and waved back. Elias yelled out, "Hello!" Brannagh blushed, and with a soft giggle, she answered, "Hi, I'm Brannagh." As the wagon traveled past her, Elias turned in his seat, and cupped both hands to the sides of his mouth. "I'm Elias. Pleasure to meet you!"

Young Elias was smitten, and soon made himself available for hire to neighboring farmers, securing not only a small income, but an opportunity to develop a friendship with Brannagh. He splurged on hard candies to share with her during their brief visits together. A small token of affection, considering her well-to-do father could afford anything her heart desired.

By eighteen, Elias had made a name for himself as an able and dependable hand, which won him the respect of Mr. Dempsey. Elias had also acquired a nice savings by then, and when he asked for Brannagh's hand in marriage, her father consented without hesitation.

As a wedding gift, the parents of the bride presented the couple with a farm. The land, located about twenty miles outside of Tahlequah, was where Grandma Janie and her younger brother Ted, were born and raised. Elias and Brannagh worked hard all their lives to make the farm both beautiful and successful. Determined to keep the property in their family, they willed it to be divided equally between their two children.

Grandma and our Great-Uncle Ted raised their families on the land. Over the years, they cultivated wheat, tobacco, cotton and maize. A tract of woods divided their acreage, but there was no need for a fence to separate their properties. Uncle Ted, as we called him, and his wife Lillian raised two children, Paul and Kathryn. After high school, both went on to attend college in Texas, where they chose to remain. Lillian passed away in her late forties, before I was born. Though his children rarely visited, Uncle Ted traveled to see them on occasion.

Grandma Janie and Jakob Samuels wed in their late teens, and were blessed with three daughters. There was Katie, the firstborn and Gunner's mom, then my mother Anna Belle, and finally Julia, who's Mitch's mom. Once adults, they eventually married and made homes within a few miles of the family farm. Oddly, each bore one child apiece.

My cousins and I were close in age, and since we lived nearby, it was convenient to spend time with Grandma Janie. I remember how excited we became when the sun turned the fields to gold, which meant it was almost television time with Grandma. After she popped a large bowl of popcorn, we'd carry our Dr. Peppers to the living room and settle together on the sofa. We enjoyed watching funny sitcoms, or sometimes a movie. To prevent the inevitable fight or spill, Grandma insisted on holding the popcorn bowl herself.

If we were still awake when the show was over, Grandma often treated us to bedtime stories about her childhood. We loved hearing about the old days, and her life on the farm. Afterward, she tucked us snuggly into fluffy down mattresses, where we slept until the rooster's crow or close to it.

I usually woke before the boys, and followed the aroma of freshly-brewed coffee straight to the kitchen. Grandma often had a pot of steaming oats on the stove, and served them up with honey and cream. She always greeted me with "good morning," and placed a glass of milk in front of me, which made me feel very special. Sunday mornings were the best. After Mitch and Gunner roused from their beds, it was time to eat and get ready for church. The place became a real madhouse as we all rushed around.

"*Nula!*" Grandma called out to us in Cherokee, meaning hurry. "We can't be late for the sermon. Gunner, please polish your dress shoes and help Mitch with his."

Gunner opened the desk drawer and removed Granddad's polish kit. With a spit and a few swipes of the cloth, their shoes shined like new. As for myself, I rummaged through every compartment of Grandma's jewelry box in search of the most colorful clip-on earrings. I held them up for her to see. "You should wear these to church, Grandma Janie."

She turned to look at me, "Sara Elizabeth Ryan, why haven't you brushed your hair? It looks like a rat's nest! Go grab the brush and bring it to me."

My cousins laughed as I ran past. Their teasing chants trailed behind me, "Sara has a rat's nest, Sara has a rat's nest."

After I was ready for church, I headed to the large front porch where I stood lookout for Uncle Ted. I skipped from one white pillar to the next, with frequent stops to pet "Momma," a yellow tabby cat who lounged lazily on the porch swing.

Grandma's farm was located on a narrow gravel road, Blackberry Lane, which branched off the main road that led into town. Blackberry Lane got its name one day as my cousins and I were picking blackberries along the fencerow. The boys did the picking, while I held the bucket. Suddenly, a shiny black car slowed and stopped. A bald man in a suit rolled down his window and peered at us over his glasses. "Hey kids! What's the name of this road?"

We all looked at one another, unsure of what to say. Gunner, the oldest at eight, stepped forward, "Which road, sir?"

The man looked up from his map and snapped, "There's only one road here, son."

Mitch, six years old and always game for an argument, cocked his head to one side and pointed to the lane behind us. "No there ain't, Mister, there's two roads."

The stranger cursed under his breath. "Oh hell, if you say so. But I need street names. Can you help me with that?"

Gunner looked over his shoulder and smiled at us, then helped as best he could, "Yes, the little one is called Blackberry Lane. The big one is called the Main Road."

The man straightened his glasses to study the wrinkled map. "Main Road? It's not on my map. And I don't see Blackberry Lane, either. Are you sure about that?"

Gunner kicked at the dirt and stifled his laugh. Mitch squinted and gave the man a berry-stained smile, "Yep, we're sure," he answered. "Hey, are you one of those insurance salesmen? My Grandma said she'd rather be kicked than talk to you people."

The irritated stranger rolled his eyes, slung the road map to the side and stomped the gas pedal. We ran to tell Grandma Janie about the encounter. She thought for a few moments before speaking. "Blackberry Lane? I like it." From that day forward, the name stuck.

I stopped skipping when I detected the sound of my uncle's Ford pickup. I called out, "Here comes Uncle Ted! He's here!"

Grandma Janie had never learned to drive, so Ted always took us to church. As we traveled along, he and Grandma held their usual Sunday conversation. He asked how she was feeling, and she answered, "Just fine, what about you?" He nodded his head and complained about the dry, wet, cold or hot weather.

The moment we arrived at church, everyone bailed out, with the exception of Uncle Ted. Right on schedule, Grandma Janie paused before closing the pickup door. "Are you sure you won't join us today, brother?"

But, as always, he tipped his cowboy hat and declined, before being on his way.

"Is Uncle Ted being foolish again?" I asked innocently.

Although she covered her mouth, I could tell she wanted to laugh. "Come along." She took hold of my hand and led us up the church sidewalk.

The preacher, Brother Jasper, nodded as we entered. I often wondered why we referred to him as a brother, because he wasn't related to us at all. We scanned the church for my Momma, who wasn't hard to spot in her floral dress, fanning her face with a lace fan. She and Aunt Katie always saved a place for us to sit.

Within minutes it seemed, my cousins and I became restless; scooting around, whispering to one another, and wiggling. Grandma Janie was prepared, though. She dug to the bottom of her large purse for a bag of Lemon Drop candies.

Gunner wasn't a fan of lemon flavors, but accepted the candy anyway. He popped one in his mouth, squinched his eyelids and drew in his cheeks. I broke into an uncontrollable giggle, which quickly led to a firm pinch on my upper arm, inflicted by Momma or Grandma, whoever was closest. And if that failed to stop my laughter, there was always Plan B; a trip to the bathroom for a harsh scolding.

Once the candies were gone, Grandma relied on a package of Juicy Fruit gum. My cousins and I knew that if we made it through an entire sermon without so much as a dirty look from our elders, we could expect to be highly praised afterward. It was in this little country church, that we learned about the importance of good manners and the life of Jesus Christ.

Grandma Janie had her work cut out for her with Mitch, though. His demeanor since birth had been unruly and temperamental. I asked Momma once why he got into so much trouble, but she made excuses for him. "It's not entirely Mitch's fault. Your Aunt Julia doesn't discipline him, and allows him do as he pleases."

This seemed to be a common topic of discussion for Mom and Aunt Katie. They often spoke in hushed tones about the way their younger sister lived her life. After losing her husband, J.D. Kincaid, in an auto accident, Julia struggled to accept reality, and soon developed a dependence on what I overheard to be "nerve pills".

Not only that, but a few short months after Uncle J.D.'s death, Julia sought solace from her loneliness in the local bars, and sometimes rough ones at that. She became involved with a few men, some of them married. Rumors and gossip ran rampant about the visitors seen leaving her home in the early morning hours.

After hearing the rumor mill, Grandma Janie questioned young Mitch, who confirmed it. He was confused by all the changes in their household. Though reluctant to intrude, Grandma finally confronted Julia, who attempted to brush it off. But that didn't work with Grandma.

"The pain isn't yours alone. Mitch is in mourning, as well. How you handle grief is your own business, but I don't want Mitch around these strangers. Bring him to me or one of your sisters before exposing him to the men you hang out with. Promise?"

Though Aunt Julia had the support of our family, with few signs of her improvement, patience wore thin. I sometimes overheard Grandma's nightly prayers, asking for Julia's comfort and healing.

Quite often it was Uncle Ted who came to Julia's rescue. On many nights, he picked her up when she was unable to drive home from the bar. He also cooked for her and Mitch when she was sick and hungover. "Who's to say what they would do in her shoes?" he said. "People handle grief in different ways."

Ted Red Eagle was known to be the life of the party, and was no stranger to the bottle himself. Aside from farming, he had also worked in the timber industry until retirement. Since then, he liked to concentrate on his favorite pastimes; like fishing with his buddies, sipping adult beverages, and doting on his 3 beloved Appaloosas. Spirit, Lady and Aspen, who he referred to as his "babies," were given the tenderest of care. My cousins and I loved them as well.

Spirit, a bay, or reddish brown in color, was born with a white blaze running down her face, and a spattering of small white spots across her hips. She had the most incredible pale blue eyes. Though very beautiful, she was stubborn as a mule, and besides Uncle Ted, the only one who could handle her was Mitch.

Lady, described by our uncle as a "Blue Roan," was actually white. Assorted black spots of all shapes and sizes scattered her entire body. She was friendly and gentle, and my favorite to ride.

Then there was Aspen, who was a mottled gray color with white stocking markings on her hind legs. Gunner was partial to her; and the two of them had been close since he was old enough to ride.

My uncle found the Appaloosa breed to be intelligent and unique, and he was certain that his horses understood every word he said. Their human-like eyes followed his every move, which indicated a clear and mutual love between horse and owner.

He often brought them along to Grandma's place. A morning ride to the pond with Mitch and Gunner, fishing poles in hand, was his idea of a perfect day. Sometimes he left the horses for the weekend, so we could ride as we pleased. Before I was old enough to ride alone, I sat on the saddle behind one of the boys, who were taught to be protective of me. On most days I didn't mind so much. Grandma and Uncle Ted were close, and they encouraged us to be close, as well.

Our grandma often gathered us around the kitchen table for what she called "lessons." She whipped up some homemade biscuits as she shared her wisdom. "You kids need to love and take care of each other. Even the Good

Book says we must be our brothers' keepers. Do you know what that means?" She studied us over her glasses.

Mitch and I shook our heads, but Gunner spoke up right away, his mouth full of bacon.

"I know, it means if I watch over them, they're supposed to watch over me. Right?"

Grandma smiled approvingly, but I was confused. "Mitch and Gunner are bigger than me. How am I supposed to take care of them?"

Grandma contemplated my question while patting out the biscuits. "There are many ways, I guess. You can cheer them up when they're sad or pray for them if they're sick. You can listen when they're upset… Or defend them, if needed. Most importantly, always let them know you love them."

Pretending to understand the importance of the lesson, I looked at the boys with a mischievous grin. Mitch stuck his tongue out at me and we exploded into laughter. Grandma touched each of our noses with a flour-dipped finger. "Go collect the eggs while I finish up these biscuits."

Gunner stalled, "Grandma, are you going to make gravy, too?"

"Well, I believe that's a possibility. Now run along and get your chores done.

I despised chickens and would go to great lengths to get out of egg gathering. My cousins, on the other hand, loved it. We grabbed our baskets and skipped across the back yard to the chicken coup. The boys paid no mind to pushing a hen off her nest, but it didn't work out so well for me and I usually got pecked or, even worse, flogged. The hen swatted me about the face and body with her wings, which sent my cousins into uproarious laughter. Mitch always rushed me, and when I began to whine, he lost his patience. "You're such a sissy. Hurry up, dammit'!"

One time I dropped the basket, stomped my foot and glared at him. "You shut your mouth. You're not the boss of me!"

He charged up to me. "You're not doing your share, Sara!"

But I held my ground. "If you don't leave me alone, I'll tell on you for saying a cuss word!"

Gunner quickly stepped between us. "Stop it, you two." he ordered, and picked up my basket. "Just wait on the porch, Sara. I'll gather them."

I overheard Mitch's objections as I walked away. "Why are you helping her, Gunner? It's not fair."

Always the gentleman, Gunner made excuses for me. "She's small and the chickens scare her. Besides, I don't mind helping."

I was at my happiest while playing with Raggedy Ann dolls, or following Grandma around all day. Sometimes I tagged along with the boys for a horseback ride to the pond. One day, I had a change of mind on the way. We'd just approached the big oak, which stood halfway between Grandma's house and the pond. I loved to play around the tree, with its large crooked limbs that dipped to touch the ground. I was riding behind Mitch, so I squeezed his ribs. "Stop! Let me off here."

Gunner, who was riding Aspen and leading Lady, came to an abrupt halt. "No, you're supposed to stay with us. That's the rule."

I dug my nails into Mitch's back. "I have to pee. Besides, I don't want to go fishing no more."

Mitch wiggled from my clutch and jumped off Spirit's back. He took a step backward and looked me over. "Why do you always change your mind about everything?"

"Help me down." I demanded.

He rolled his eyes and extended a hand. "Let's just go," he said to Gunner. "She'll be all right."

"Well, you can take the blame if she falls out of the tree and gets hurt."

Mitch studied Gunner, then gave me a hard look. "Just stay on the low limbs, okay?"

I crossed my legs and held myself. "Go on!"

Before they rode away, Gunner issued my orders. "Next time, make sure to clear it with Grandma first. And no matter what, don't go wandering off. Stay right here. We'll be back to pick you up in a little while."

I enjoyed being alone with the tree. After a fair amount of climbing and exploring, I soon nestled into the hollow of its trunk. I knew Grandma might disapprove of my being alone, but what could possibly go wrong out here? I'd be in greater danger at the pond, where I could possibly drown or be bitten by a snake.

I gazed up at the sunbeams flickering through the leaves. A soft breeze blew my damp curls, my eyelids grew heavy, and I began to doze off. It seemed like only a few seconds when I was jolted awake by a rumble. It was so loud; it shook the ground beneath me.

Afternoon thunderstorms were common here in Tornado Alley. Some were mild and ended quickly. Others required a dash to the concrete storm cellar. Almost everyone living in these parts had one in their backyard. There wasn't much Grandma Janie was afraid of, but she was terrified of storms. We dared not argue with her about going to the dark, creepy cellar. She always grabbed her coal oil lantern on the way out the door, saying something like, "I've seen many a storm in my day, and it's better to be safe than sorry."

The sky grew increasingly dark and menacing. I scanned the land, but couldn't see the boys. The wind picked up enough speed to sway the top of the massive tree. Panic began to set in. I could barely see the roof of Grandma's house, but her voice carried faintly on the wind as she cried out, "You kids need to come home now!"

The wind blew harder, and I clutched a limb for dear life. It was hard to see through blowing dust, but I made out my cousins as they chased the horses. Mitch lunged for Aspen's reins, but she bolted from his grip. Just as Gunner reached Spirit, she reared as he tried to mount her, sending him tumbling. After another loud clap of thunder, all three horses ran off together.

Gunner yelled to me. "Sara, get away from the tree!"

I let go of the limb and ran. The lightning was closer and seemed to strike upon my heels as I raced to my cousins. Wind swept the rain in sheets across the field, flattening the tall grass against the Earth. I stumbled over a tree root and fell hard. I struggled back to my feet and began to cry. My knees burned, and blood ran down each leg, soaking into my socks. Gunner and Mitch battled against the wind, and were out of breath when they reached me. Gunner seized one of my hands, as Mitch took the other. "Let's go to our fort," Gunner said. "It's close." I held on tightly as we ran to a nearby patch of woods.

I'd never been inside their fort. They built it with the help of Lucas Crow, their friend who lived down the road. Until today, I was told that girls were "never, ever, ever allowed inside."

Mitch opened the makeshift door and Gunner led me inside the tipi-style structure. We sat on wooden boxes as rain leaked through dead tree limbs and old scraps of lumber and tin. Although the boys felt safe there, I didn't have much confidence in the shaking heap of sticks. "I want my grandma," I bawled.

Mitch tried to comfort me. "Don't cry, Sara. The storm will be over in a little bit." Gunner patted my back and the three of us huddled together, cold, soaking wet and trembling. Thunder boomed, and suddenly the door blew off.

I looked to Mitch; his eyes were wide with terror. Just then, we noticed movement outside. The figure came closer. I screamed and buried my face in Gunner's sleeve. Lightning flashed, and I peeked between my fingers. It was Grandma. Pink apron strings flew above her head and her silver-flecked black hair whipped about, set loose from its bun. She peered in through the missing door. "Come with me. We'll wait out the storm in the barn."

We ran behind her as the storm raged around us. Grandma led us into the barn, then closed the double doors and latched them behind her. She directed us to a few bales of hay, where we sat together. I clutched Grandma Janie tight. At times I feared the roof would go. Scenes from "The Wizard of Oz" flashed through my mind.

Tears welled up in Gunner's eyes. "I'm worried about the horses, Grandma. They got away from us."

"Oh, don't fret over them. They're probably back at Ted's place by now."

Gunner wiped his tears. "We're sorry, Grandma."

"We shouldn't have left Sara." Mitch confessed. "We won't do it again."

Grandma gave us a stern look, but before she could speak, I came clean. "Don't be mad at them, Grandma. It's my fault. I didn't want to play at the pond today."

Grandma Janie didn't scold us, but she issued a quick reminder. "Remember what I have taught you. Keep watch over one another. You did a good job today, and I'm very proud."

She pulled me onto her lap, and the boys scooted in close. She did her best to comfort us.

"We'll be okay here. Your Granddad built this barn with his own hands."

And she was right; the barn held strong.

After the storm passed, we waded through puddles of water back to the house. The storm had knocked the electricity off. Grandma Janie dried us in the light of candles and her lantern, and helped us into our warm pajamas. She applied one of her homemade poultices to my knees. We were allowed to sleep with her that night. Worn out from all the excitement, we slept like babies as the rain pelted against the windows.

First thing the next morning, we inspected the farm for damage. Unfortunately, the fort didn't make it. Grandma pointed to the now-vacant spot on the ground. "You children could have been blown away. Thank Heavens I found you when I did."

Just as we settled in for breakfast, there was a knock on the front door. Grandma rose to answer it, and soon ushered Lucas Crow into the kitchen.

Lucas was soft-spoken and shy. "I tried to call, but our phone isn't working."

Grandma nodded. "Yes, the storm knocked them all out."

"I wanted to let you know about the powwow tonight."

The boys and I jumped from our chairs. "Can we go?"

Grandma waved a hand in the air. "Hold up. I'll speak to your Uncle Ted when the phone is back on. If he wants to drive us, we'll go watch Lucas perform."

Lucas was polite and kind, and Grandma considered him a great influence on Mitch and Gunner. She'd always been particular about our friends, but had known Lucas' family for years, and he was always welcome to come over and play. He and Mitch were classmates.

Lucas was very helpful when the occasional argument erupted between my cousins. He refused to choose sides, but if diplomacy should fail, he served as a convenient referee. He was often quiet for stretches of time, but his large round eyes spoke volumes. And even at my young age, I could read him easily.

Lucas had learned Native Cherokee dances from his dad and uncles, and performed them in local powwow competitions. Though he'd made several attempts to teach the dances to my cousins, they never quite caught on. Grandma and I used to sneak behind the clothesline to watch them. As Mitch and Gunner clumsily followed Lucas's instructions, she and I cupped our hands over our mouths, and giggled between the sun-bleached sheets.

I had many adventures with my cousins on the farm, but as they grew older, I was less often included. They spent more and more of their time hanging around with Lucas. He often rode his horse over to spend the day, and the three of them would roam the farm to their heart's content. They built a new fort, a more stable one this time. Sometimes they camped there overnight. Long summer days were spent fishing at the pond, or hunting and exploring in the woods.

Lucas taught my cousins how to make bird calls by cupping his hands together and blowing into them. The sound came out low and hollow, and ended with a high-pitched whistle. It was their secret signal, and served to warn each other when intruders were about. Intruders such as myself, if I happened to wander too close to their compound.

Grandma Janie was pleased to see us enjoying her farm. After raising only daughters, it was a new adventure to have three boys around. The sun had bronzed their skin, and she often referred to them as her young braves. They were easy and uncomplicated. Not once did they turn up their noses at a meal, but happily scarfed down every bite before asking for more. Grandma's only complaint was how badly they smelled after a day spent fishing. "No one goes to bed without a bath," she'd say.

Uncle Ted loved to drive us to powwows. It gave him a chance to visit with old friends there. With the five of us packed tightly into his pickup seat, we'd set off for a full day of fun, with lawn chairs and an ice chest in tow. And the closer we got to the event, the more our excitement grew.

After we helped unload the truck, the boys and I were free to roam the grounds like young hunters, so long as we stayed together. We were entranced by the spectacle of it all; the aromas wafting the air, the fervent chanting, and the deep rhythm of the drums, which Uncle Ted said represented the heartbeat of our Earth.

After locating Lucas and his family, we helped to prepare him for his performance.

"Are you nervous?" Gunner asked between bites of meat pie, a pastry filled with meat and assorted seasonings.

Lucas shook his head and pulled on his moccasins. He rose and stood before me. I was in awe of his dance regalia: outfitted with beads and fur, fringe, feathers and colored ribbons. Each piece held its own personal and sacred meaning.

After Lucas hurried off to the Grand Entry line up, my cousins and I wound our way back to camp, where Grandma had spread an old quilt onto the grass. We lounged about, and waited for the music to begin. Finally, the ceremony started and veterans and dignitaries marched by, carrying a colorful array of flags. The dancers filed in behind them. My heart raced when Lucas passed us. After that, we heard a beautiful song performed by one of the elders, and then a prayer.

We watched Lucas as he danced in the Junior Boys Grass Dance competition. He stomped and kicked in perfect time while his roach—a headpiece with Eagle feathers—rocked back and forth on his head. Legend holds that the feathers represent two brothers who were separated as children, but found each other later in life, reunited by the dance.

Although quite aware of my heritage, watching Lucas made it all the more real. The dancers filed past with Mother Wind in their feathered bustles. The night air was alive with mystery as the spiritual and physical worlds connected.

After the ceremony wore down, we bid Lucas and his family good night, then packed up to head home. The boys and I were still wound up from the excitement, and had a million questions for the drive back to Waya.

"I didn't see very many white people there." Mitch concluded.

"You're white." Uncle Ted laughed.

"More white folks come to powwows than they used to, right brother?" Grandma said.

"Why?" Mitch asked.

Uncle Ted answered. "A long time ago, when your grandmother and I were young, Indians weren't allowed to throw powwows as often as we do today. The government limited how many we could hold within a year."

Again, Mitch asked why.

Grandma attempted to explain. "People are often scared of what they don't understand. Our sacred dances were regarded as pagan rituals."

Gunner interrupted. "What does pagan mean?"

Grandma continued. "Someone who follows a religion based on nature. Some Pagans don't necessarily worship just one God."

Uncle Ted cut right through it. "Folks used to think our ways were like voodoo, but the truth is, we pray to the same God. God has many names, you know."

I was thoroughly confused, but my cousins were increasingly curious.

Grandma did her best to keep the conversation on our level. "Yes, names such as the Great Spirit, or Creator. A long time ago, our ancestors worshiped differently than the missionaries who came here to convert them. It caused fear, so the missionaries attempted to make it harder for us to worship. But things are better now, right Ted? We're free to hold ceremonies as we please."

I finally had a question of my own. "Why you don't go to church with us, Uncle Ted?"

He chuckled, "Don't worry about me, baby. I believe in God. I talk with Him every day. But my religion is a private thing. I'm truer to the old ways."

After a few minutes of silence, Mitch and Gunner nodded off. But I remained wide-eyed from the day's events. I leaned my head on Gunner's shoulder and wondered if Lucas was still awake, too. Grandma and Uncle Ted spoke softly, sometimes in Cherokee, which I didn't understand.

Grandma giggled at one point, and teased her brother. "I held my breath for a few minutes there," she told him. "I thought you were going to mention Peyotism. Boy, would I have had a time explaining that."

Uncle Ted nodded. "They'll eventually hear about the Native American Church, sister. It was developed in Oklahoma, after all."

"Yes, I'm sure."

"Another misinterpretation from the past is about peyote, and that it is used with an intent to get high. But it's only a sacrament. Our elders believed that all plants had a purpose and—if used safely—could serve us in body or spirit."

Grandma smiled. "Yes, indeed," she said. "I haven't partaken, but the elders say it strengthens the bond between us and God."

Uncle Ted seemed deep in his thoughts, before sharing them. "Some say peyote is dangerous."

"Anything can be dangerous if misused," Grandma said. She must have felt my eyes upon her, and quickly looked down at me. "Are you eavesdropping, granddaughter?"

I shook my head.

"Tell me the truth," she said.

I nodded.

"I have noticed you doing this lately. Okay, then." She patted my thigh. "Since you're curious, I promise to teach you about our native customs and medicines. And you will also learn to speak our language. These things are important and must be passed down. It might as well be to you."

With each powwow, I learned more about our tribal traditions, which were important to Grandma Janie. Our family also had its private traditions. We celebrated birthdays and holidays simply, yet Grandma went all out with her cooking and baking abilities. To honor our events, she made dishes that were passed down from generation to generation. Many of her meals were made with venison and the Three Sisters: corn, beans and squash.

Over the years, Grandma and her daughters developed a unique cooking style of their own, a fusion of Cherokee, Irish, and Old South. Their creations served our community—to cheer, to soothe, or to welcome. On family birthdays, we were presented with our favorite cake or pie. Get togethers were loud, filled with laughter, and—if Grandma had anything to do with it—devoid of alcohol. "That stuff is of the Devil," she claimed, "And a family event is no place for it."

Grandma despised what my Aunt Julia was doing to herself.

I recall a particular Friday evening when I was twelve years old. Grandma and I were in her kitchen. We both jumped as the screen door slammed. It was Mitch coming in.

Grandma scolded, "What have I told you about slamming that screen?"

He apologized quickly. We loved Grandma dearly, and didn't enjoy being on her bad side. After helping himself to a glass of milk, Mitch sat down at the table and sniffed the air.

"What are y'all cookin'?"

I was quick to announce the menu. "Shepherd's pie, and corn on the cob from the garden."

"And yeast rolls, too." Grandma Janie raised her eyebrows. "You hungry?"

Mitch avoided her stare, but nodded as he gazed out the window.

"How's your Momma today?" Grandma asked, maybe from intuition.

Mitch swigged his last gulp of milk before answering.

"Sleeping. I had to take her to the ER early this morning."

Grandma Janie turned the burners to low, wiped her hands on a towel, and then sat next to him. "Tell me what happened, *ulisi atsutsa*," she said, meaning "Grandson" in Cherokee.

He struggled to fight something back, but whether tears or anger, I couldn't tell.

"I heard a loud noise around 3 a.m. and found her on the living room floor. I guess she passed out and bumped her head on the way down."

"Pills or liquor?" Grandma asked.

Mitch looked her in the eye. "Pills this time. Doctor said to let her sleep it off. She must have taken her doses too close together and it made her wobbly."

Grandma pulled him in for a hug. "I'll talk to her later. Unfortunately, she needs more help than I can give her. And that doctor of hers needs to be ran out of town." She attempted to reign in her frustration, but I could hear it in her voice. She dabbed her eyes with a towel before returning to the stove.

"How did you get here?" I asked him. "Did you walk?"

"Nope, I drove Mom's car." he said proudly.

"You drove without an adult in the car? But you only have a permit."

His stare cut right through me.

Grandma turned to give him that familiar look of hers. The same one she used when we misbehaved in church. "Don't make a habit of taking her car. Got it?"

He nodded. She giggled and swatted him with a tea towel. "Grab your plates, kids. Supper's ready. If you're staying for a while, I can make us some popcorn balls later."

Mitch and I grinned from ear to ear at the mention of Grandma's popcorn balls, a gooey treat that she usually reserved for Halloween. Later that night, she asked Mitch to drive us to check on Aunt Julia. We took her a warm meal and made sure she was steady on her feet again. Then Uncle Ted came to drive me and Grandma back to the farm. He weighed in on things as we drove along. "I'd like to knock the hell out of that doctor of hers. What's he thinking, giving her all that dope?"

Grandma nodded, "Mm-hm. I'm calling his office on Monday. He'll get a piece of my mind."

"He never listens," Ted growled. "Bastard needs to be turned in to the authorities."

That was only the beginning of Julia's close calls. When her doctor finally cut her off, she found another to oblige, and then another. Over the next two years, she drifted further into her own self-destruction. Julia eventually isolated herself, despite pleas from Mitch and everyone else. She even missed Gunner's high school graduation, which left Aunt Katie sorely disappointed.

Grandma Janie worried incessantly about Julia's condition, and did everything she could to help. Intuition warned her that the situation was dire and ill-fated. One night, after hearing an owl's call from a nearby tree, Grandma feared the worse. Cherokee superstition held that the sighting of a nearby owl foretold of bad fortune.

I heard her tell Uncle Ted about the owl's sighting. "It was there." She pointed to the lowest limb of a Hickory tree. "I've never seen an owl in my yard before."

Uncle Ted shook his head. "Janie, I don't want to believe that."

But soon they had no choice.

It happened one week after Mitch's seventeenth birthday. He found Julia in their backyard, unresponsive. He rushed to call Uncle Ted, because the closest ambulance was almost twenty miles away. They loaded her into Ted's truck and sped to the hospital. Julia was admitted to ICU and placed on a ventilator. Two days later, her condition hadn't improved.

Finally, the doctor ordered an EEG test to check for brain activity. There wasn't any. He then asked the family to make a hard decision: keep her on the ventilator and hope for a miracle, or unplug it to end her life. Uncle Ted abruptly left the waiting room. I'll never forget the pain in his sobs as they echoed down the long hospital hallway.

The most memorable thing about Julia's death, was the absence of shock and disbelief. Her fate was accepted, and if discussed, only briefly. Momma and Aunt Katie made the necessary arrangements. Four days later, Julia was laid to rest in our family plot high on Cemetery Hill. Mitch was silent and withdrawn throughout the service. Gunner never left his side that day.

Mitch moved in with Grandma Janie right away. Aunt Julia's property was sold, except for her candy-apple red 1967 Thunderbird, which Mitch kept. All proceeds went to Grandma, who was left with Mitch's upbringing. Gunner searched for ways to distract Mitch from his grief.

"Let me try to get you and Lucas on at the feed store. We could use more help. What do you say?" Gunner asked. He had worked at Horizon Livestock Feeds since graduation, and it was only a short drive away. "

Mitch shrugged. "Yeah, that sounds cool, I guess."

Grandma teased. "The three of you working together? You'll be thick as thieves again."

For one so young, Mitch had suffered his share of loss. Now, in 1972 and his senior year of high school, he jumped at the chance to sow some proverbial wild oats. Often moody and aloof, he grew his hair long, and chose to hang out with a different crowd.

The rest of us trained our energy on another tradition, the large summer garden to be planted on Grandma's farm. Since we all lived close, the work was easily shared. Gardening served as a much-needed therapy. My dad, James, along with Gunner's father, Stan, took tiller duties. Once the rows of dirt were prepared, the planting took place. Uncle Ted was on hand to help, mostly by issuing orders. "Don't plant the peas too close together." he advised.

For my grandmother, Mom, and Aunt Katie, digging and nurturing plants helped them with their grief. Fruits and vegetables sprung forth with an abundance, and were shared with friends and neighbors. "We have tomatoes coming out of our ears," Mom said.

As a teenager, playing in the dirt no longer interested me. My mind was on other things, like spending time with my best friend, Gillian Farrell, or "Gillie", as she was called. We'd known each other since grade school, and our families were members of the same church. But there was no fun for me until my gardening chores were tended to each day, such as washing, peeling and chopping the produce. One morning, Aunt Katie arrived late for garden duty. I glanced out the window and saw her bolt up the rock pathway to Grandma's porch, then she stopped short of the screen door. She hesitated for a few seconds, then stepped into the living room. When she removed her stylish sunglasses, her eyes were red and swollen. No doubt she'd been crying.

"What's wrong?" Grandma asked.

Katie collapsed into the nearest chair. "I just don't know how much more I can stand, Momma. Gunner received a draft notice."

The Vietnam War was a world away, but seemed to loom over every American household. For years, Grandma had often voiced her concerns about the drawn-out war. Now I knew why.

After Aunt Katie's announcement, Grandma walked out the door and to a corner of the porch, the same spot where she summoned us home when we were little. She leaned against a pillar and gazed across the field. Mom discussed the details with my aunt, but I couldn't concentrate on a word they were saying.

The thought of Gunner going so far away troubled me. The following days, I sought ways to escape reality. I discovered the comfort of music. During sleepovers at Gillie's house, we listened to stacks of her older sister, Paulette's albums. We also thumbed through rock magazines, like "Creem" and "Circus." Evenings were spent down at the creek on her family's property, swimming and sunning ourselves. A savage tan was a must-have before returning to school in the fall. My days were warm and easy, despite the dread of Gunner's upcoming deployment. Mom and Grandma made arrangements for his send-off party. Mitch, Lucas, and I volunteered to help.

"Gunner's departure isn't something I prefer to celebrate," Grandma told me. "But we'll throw him a nice party and see him off with a great meal."

Three weeks later, the party began at noon. It was a beautiful day, without a cloud in sight. Lucas and Mitch began a lengthy game of horseshoes. Uncle Ted brought the Appaloosas over, and constructed a makeshift bar out by the barn. "Take Me Back to Tulsa," a Bob Wells & His Texas Playboys tune, blared from a radio.

The sweet, rich aromas of BBQ and blackberry cobbler drifted on the air. Neighbors, friends and family filed in and out for hours. Gunner had several female visitors, too. I watched each tearful goodbye, and dreaded ours more by the minute.

Gunner was somewhat popular around town. He was the strong silent type, and blessed with good looks and a warm personality. He had dark hair and olive skin like Mitch, but Gunner's features were more rugged, with a thick nose and square jaw. His smile was wide and generous. He was tall and slightly stout, like his dad, Stan Lane. Easygoing and uncomplicated, Gunner disliked even the hint of drama. Emotional outbursts made him ill-at-ease. "This shit is getting way too deep," he was known to say.

But on this day, Gunner made himself tolerant of the tears and mushiness. He issued hugs, handshakes and kisses. He took down addresses and promised to write. He listened to war stories from the older vets, and beamed happily with each pat on the back. He said a goodbye to each Appaloosa, and promised Aspen he'd be home again soon.

Right after midnight, Gunner walked into the kitchen. He looked down at the floor and hesitated a moment. Aunt Katie blinked back tears, as Uncle Stan took her hand in his. We all gathered round. Gunner cleared his throat before speaking.

"It's late, and I've gotta' hit the road early. This was a great party and I appreciate everything." He swallowed hard. "Try not to worry about me. I'll be all right." He hugged us one by one. "Don't grow up too fast." he teased me. "I won't be around to keep an eye on you, but I have my informants. I'll write as soon as I can."

I couldn't speak for the giant lump in my throat. I hugged him tighter, reluctant to let go.

He then moved on to Grandma Janie. "*Donadagohvi*," she spoke through tears, which means 'til we meet again.' Looking up into his eyes, she continued. "Let my lessons guide you, and if you become worried or scared, just read this scripture out loud." She handed him a folded piece of paper. "I love you, *ulisi atsutsa*."

Gunner kissed her forehead. "I love you, Grandma."

I watched through the screen door when Mitch and Lucas walked him out. They kidded and poked fun at him, and did their best to make him laugh. Then Gunner shook Lucas's hand, and they exchanged farewells. After Gunner shut the car door, Mitch leaned in. "Hey, don't let 'em creep up on you. Use those hunting instincts."

"I will," Gunner said. "You take care, man… And don't do anything stupid."

"I'll keep myself busy with consoling your girlfriends," Mitch teased.

Gunner laughed and drove away.

Lucas jumped on the porch and sat in the swing. Mitch stood alone in the driveway, and watched until Gunner's taillights disappeared. The lonely call of a bob white bird sounded in the distance. I slipped out the door and sat beside Lucas. His large eyes searched mine. Too sad to speak, we sat in the darkness, my head on his shoulder.

Summer slipped into fall. Mitch said little about it, but there were times I could tell he missed his parents and Gunner. Like the evenings when he sat alone, strumming Jim Croce songs on a secondhand guitar. As the months passed, I saw less and less of him. Most often it was as he breezed by on his way out the door; his hair slicked back, still wet from the shower. The scent of Irish Spring soap lingered behind him.

Grandma Janie began to hear rumors about Mitch's excessive partying, but refrained from nagging at him.

"Hopefully just a phase." she told Uncle Ted, who wasn't so sure.

"It's probably those new pals of his," Uncle Ted said. "They're bad company. I heard that Mitch is being a real smartass lately. His boss, Jim, down at the feed store told me he puts Mitch in check on a regular basis. I drove by the Piggly Wiggly one evening and saw Mitch and his buddies hanging out in the parking lot. Mitch was stretched out on the hood of his car, swigging on a bottle of Jack Daniels. I should've stopped and said something, but who am I to talk?"

Grandma kept her eyes trained on her crocheting project. "Exactly. Mitch has always looked up to you, though."

Puzzled, Ted took off his cowboy hat and waved it around. "Now why the hell would he look up to me?"

Grandma shrugged her shoulders, then seized an opportunity for a little good-natured ribbing. "Maybe because both of you like to drink and kick up the dust?"

Uncle Ted's expression seemed unsure of whether he had been complimented or insulted. I struggled to hold my tongue, but soon gave in. "Mitch says you're the best horseman he knows, and that you can drink anyone in Cherokee County under the table."

Grandma snickered.

Uncle Ted stammered a little. "Uh, that's just bullshit… Well, maybe in my younger days."

Unable to concentrate, Grandma pushed the ball of yarn aside. "Be proud, little brother. You can hold your liquor, and that's a fine asset."

In addition to partying, Mitch was quite the ladies' man. I'd never welcomed the thought of sharing Mitch or Gunner. In my eyes, there wasn't a worthy female on Earth for them, and I tended to greet their girlfriends with a wall of jealousy. One evening, Mitch brought an unfamiliar guest to our southern-style fish fry supper. Valerie Cantrell, who was new in town, beamed like the sun as Mitch took her around for the introductions.

Gillie and I, perched upon a fence rail, were quick to give her the once-over. "She's so disco," Gillie whispered. "I love her outfit."

I immediately noticed Valerie's beauty. Blonde, tanned, and styled to perfection. Despite my plan to remain unimpressed, her sweet smile and personality soon won me over. By evening's end, she'd shown me and Gillie how to wing out our hair, Farrah Fawcett-style. She also took blue eye shadow from her bag and let us try it on. We discussed music, and Valerie recommended the new Donna Summer album. She seemed to fit right in, so I gave Mitch a discreet nod of approval. He nodded back and winked, which made me feel as if my opinion mattered.

A few weeks after Gunner left, letters came to us from Fort Polk, Louisiana. Mine actually arrived in its own envelope, and separate from the one he sent to Mom and Dad. I ran to my bedroom and ripped it open, hoping to read of new adventures outside of our ho-hum town. Gunner explained that basic training was much harder than he'd ever imagined. Once he had it under his belt, he'd be heading overseas. He wrote about the Louisiana humidity, describing it much like a hot, wet blanket clinging to his body. But he claimed the experience would prepare him for the Vietnam climate. "I hope you've been gathering those eggs for Grandma," he teased.

His letter was comforting, albeit short. I didn't watch the news often, but had heard of the possible horrors he might face. He told me to expect another letter soon, and signed off with, "P.S. Promise to always be a good kid."

Later that day, I caught a ride to Grandma's house with Uncle Ted. Grandma Janie had prepared her delicious goulash. I finished my meal, except for a small pile of chopped green peppers left hidden under my napkin. Afterwards, we sat in front of the TV and watched the world news, which consisted mostly of reports on the war. Grandma soon turned it off. "Did you get letters?" she asked us.

My uncle and I both nodded. I told them about mine with wide-eyed excitement; it was my first letter ever. Uncle Ted remained quiet. Eventually, he grabbed his hat and thanked Grandma for supper. She and I walked him to the porch. Ted stopped on the top step, then turned. "They need to do away with that dad-gummed draft," he said. "It targets the poor. Hell, we've already lost this war. What are those kids dying for anyway?"

TWO

The Foxhole

During Gunner's time in Vietnam, I was intent on becoming the teenager of my dreams. My social life developed, which unfortunately affected the amount of time I normally spent with Grandma Janie. At fifteen, and still too young to date, Gillie and I threw ourselves into the customary teenaged pastimes of music, fashion, and boy-talk.

The music of the 1970s exploded in every genre from easy listening to disco. I developed a hunger, and bought up new albums as fast as my allowance could afford. I didn't want to miss a thing, and slept with a transistor radio to my ear, tuned to an awesome rock station in Kansas City. Since we lived out in the boonies, getting a clear transmission was a challenge. I looked forward to the day I would have a driver's license, and be free to attend music festivals and concerts.

With Mitch gone most of the time, Grandma Janie's house was quieter than ever. Sometimes when I was there, I'd stroll across the field to the big oak. My eyes searched the familiar land, but the excitement I had as a child was gone and replaced with a deep void.

Some things remained unchanged. Uncle Ted still picked me and Grandma up for church on Sundays. But he stopped bringing the Appaloosas over. He developed a herniated disc in his back, and didn't ride them anymore. Now, the horses grazed around in the field, and greeted him for grain and a brushing each evening. After he tucked them lovingly into their stalls, Uncle Ted turned in early, sometimes even before dark.

He once explained why the Appaloosa breed was so special to him. Though known for beauty and extraordinary strength, it was their history that impressed him the most. Appaloosas were bred by the Nez Perce people of the Pacific Northwest, essentially for use in farming and buffalo hunting. In 1877, tensions rose with the U.S. Army. Upset by a land treaty dispute, Nez Perce Chief Joseph formed a coalition with other Indian leaders who were determined to remain on their ancestral lands.

After persistent pressure by the Army, the Nez Perce were forced to flee their homeland. They traveled to Montana Territory with hopes of uniting with the Crow tribe, but were turned away upon arrival. With a new plan to seek sanctuary with the Lakota, Chief Joseph changed the course to Canada. The Appaloosas valiantly carried his people along the journey of over 1,100 miles, with Army soldiers in pursuit. Skirmishes broke out along the way. Although the Nez Perce tribe won several of these conflicts, many of their warriors became injured or worn down. As the weather deteriorated, there were many deaths due to exposure. Determined to make it to the Canadian border, they pushed onward, fully confident in the strength and endurance of the Appaloosas.

When the Army closed in, the Nez Perce War erupted. The weather was freezing, and with no blankets and little food, Chief Joseph chose what was best for his people. On October 5th, 1877, he rode up the hill at Bear Paw Battlefield, Montana and surrendered--forty miles short of the Canadian border. "Hear me, my chiefs: My heart is sick and sad. From where the Sun now stands, I will fight no more forever," he said.

After his surrender, Chief Joseph and many of his followers were sent to Fort Leavenworth in Kansas, and then eventually to Indian Territory. The Army confiscated over 1000 of his surviving horses. Some were sold, and the rest were shot. Due to the slaughter, the Appaloosas fell into near extinction until the 1930s. But, our uncle explained, with the strength and perseverance bred in them by the Nez Perce people, the breed pulled through and flourished again.

The winter of 1974 was unusually long, with dark days, bitter winds and snow. Uncle Ted slipped and fell on a patch of ice, which further aggravated his back condition. He underwent surgery, and after his discharge, we all pulled together to help him.

Mitch was hired at the lumber mill during his final months of high school; a definite step up from the feed store. The mill, being the largest employer in town, of-fered better pay and benefits. My dad, an employee for many years, always said a job at the mill was as good as gold. Mitch sold his Thunderbird to my mom, and bought a used Ford pickup. His relationship with Valerie was se-rious, and they made plans to move in together after high school graduation.

I feared it might upset Grandma, who disapproved of couples living together outside of marriage. But to my surprise, she accepted the idea. "Mitch is eighteen now and besides, Valerie is a great influence on him. She is very level-headed, and provides the stability he needs."

Mitch took it upon himself to check on Uncle Ted every day as he recovered. He helped with projects around the house, and cared for the horses. Lucas often dropped by for a couple of beers and a card game.

As spring neared, letters from Gunner came regularly. He wrote to me about new friends he'd made, like heli-copter pilot Lance Ferguson. "He's quite the character and practically a neighbor, being from Hot Springs, Arkansas. Lance, with his crew chief, Zed and shotgun rider, Rufus are what's called a "dustoff crew." They fly medical evac-uation missions to rescue wounded soldiers. All three of them are from the South. People call them the Bayou Bad Asses, and it's even painted on the helicopter. Sometimes we drink a beer together and talk about back home. I guess you don't know how special home is until you're far away from it. When I'm out in the jungle and can't sleep, I look up at the stars and remember campouts with Mitch and Lucas. It calms me, somehow. Please give Grandma a hug, okay? Love you, Gunner."

Although I respected Gunner's opinion about our hometown, I didn't see myself remaining in Waya forever. Grandma Janie held onto hopes that her family would always live close, but I had other plans. My greatest fear, at the time, was being stuck in our one-horse town for life. I developed a love for books about travel and geography.

I had frequent daydreams of myself strolling a foreign street, exotic aromas in the air, and the strum of a gypsy guitar filling the night. I yearned for new experiences, but according to Grandma Janie, there was no better place to be than right here in the Ozark foothills.

Throughout our childhood days, my cousins and I had enjoyed frequent hikes with Grandma. A trusty walking stick in her hand, she led us along the trails and deep into the woods, teaching us about the land, its plants and their uses.

"Take a look at what grows around you. See the ginseng plants? What about the dogwood trees? Our ancestors used them in medicines. Who can point one out a persimmon tree?"

As usual, Gunner was the first to respond. He pointed, "I see one!"

She nodded, "*Osda.* They nourish our wildlife, you know."

We traveled to the water's edge. "Think about what the Illinois River does for us. Pure, clean water is necessary for good health. Not only for us, but for fish and all of nature. Water is sacred, and shall not be desecrated. That's why it's up to all us to protect it."

At times we'd venture out at night, sit on top of the cellar and study the heavens. Grandma stood with her arms outstretched, so tiny in stature, the cobalt sky as her backdrop.

"We share a kinship with the Earth and sky," she told us. "We breathe the same air, drink the same water, and are nourished by the same dirt. Balance is good medicine, and is very crucial to our happiness. When it becomes off-set, peace is lost. We can all expect a fair share of pain in our lives, it's unavoidable. If we master a balance, as the elements do, harmony will prevail."

While it was common in our community for young ladies to marry immediately after high school, I was determined to reach for different stars. And so was Gillie, for the most part. We discussed our options while lounging on fluffy pillows on her bedroom floor. A Linda Ronstadt album played on the stereo. College brochures lay scattered about.

"We should room together in college, don't you think?" I asked. "And maybe after we graduate, we can get a cool apartment. I don't plan on getting married until I'm at least 30."

"Thirty is old, Sara. Your uterus will be all dried up by then. Don't you want to have kids? I want to get married before my face is wrinkled."

I reconsidered. "You're right. I want to look great for my wedding, too. If I meet my soulmate, maybe I'll move the age down some."

"I'm not so sure I want to go to college, but you definitely should. Especially since your parents have been saving for it." Gillie rolled onto her back and stared at the ceiling. "Gosh, can you believe we'll finally be turning sixteen this summer? I wonder how old I'll be when I lose my virginity?"

The brochure I was looking over fell from my hands and to the floor. "Whoa, that was random. Do you have a prospect or something?"

Gillie giggled uncontrollably. "Oh my God, don't make me pee my pants! And you would know if I did. We're best friends, right?"

I relaxed and pulled a cherry lip gloss from her bag. "I like this color," I smeared it generously on my lips and smacked them together. "How does it look on me?"

She gave me a thumbs up and replied with a fake British accent. *"Fabulous, dah'ling."*

After a brief silence, I came clean. "It's not that I don't wonder about that stuff, Gillie. But boys seem so immature, at least the ones at school are. They're actually kind of gross."

Gillie sat up. "That's because we've been in the same classes with them since kindergarten. Paulette said guys are like octopuses. They'll try to feel you up if you're not careful. She told me that Carl Hughes jammed his tongue down her throat and grabbed a boob at the same time."

I gasped. "What happened next?"

"She called him a horn dog and stomped his big toe."

"Are you sure about that? I mean, we're talking about your sister here."

"Well, I don't know," Gillie shook her head. "But she told me that guys can be real pigs and forget their manners when you're all alone with them. I hope you and I find real gentleman to be our first…"

I interrupted her. "Yeah, for sure." I felt myself blush. "But, for now we should concentrate on an education." I pushed a brochure into her hand.

Gillie turned up her nose and tossed it aside. "First things first, though. Let's think about fun stuff. I know…Since our birthdays are only two weeks apart, we should celebrate together. What do you think?"

I nodded and smiled. "Sweet sixteen. I'll drink to that."

We clicked our Dr. Pepper bottles.

Spring brought a series of highs mixed with lows. Lucas, Valerie and Mitch graduated from high school in mid-

May. After commencement, we came back to Grandma's farm for cake and homemade ice cream. I invited Gillie, too. Later, she and I sat on lawn chairs in the front yard and waited for Paulette to pick her up. "When did Lucas become so hot," Gillie asked, "or have you even noticed?"

"Lucas? Hot? Well, I guess he's all right. Why do you ask?"

"He hasn't taken his eyes off you all night."

My mouth fell open. "Seriously? Are you sure?"

She grinned like the cat that ate the canary. "Oh yes, girl. And I think you need glasses."

I squirmed in my chair. "Well, I've always thought he was, umm, cute."

Gillie looked over each shoulder before speaking. "He might be a good prospect."

"A prospect for what?"

About that time, Lucas and Mitch walked onto the porch.

Gillie whispered, "For what we talked about a few weeks ago. You trust him, right? I think he would be a gentleman."

I didn't catch on right away. She tried not to laugh. "Sara, maybe he could show you the ropes?"

I snapped from my muddle. "What? No way. That's crazy!"

"Ssshhh..." she waved her hands.

"Who's crazy?" Mitch hollered from the porch.

"Oh, nothing," I answered.

Gillie poked me in the ribs, then leaned in closer just as Paulette drove up. "Just think about it. He really digs you; I can tell. Later, gator." She grabbed her cardigan and ran to the driveway.

As Mitch and Lucas walked toward me, I checked Lucas out more thoroughly. Gillie had a point about him looking hot, especially tonight, dressed in denim bell bottoms and a Led Zeppelin t-shirt. He had grown out his hair over the past few months, and it was neatly groomed into a short ponytail. I picked up the scent of his musky cologne. Suddenly, my lips were dry. I looked away, and reached for my soda.

"Oh, now I know what you meant." Mitch said.

I almost choked on my drink. "Ah, huh?"

"Oh, come on," Mitch said. "You two were talking about Paulette. That girl is wild *and* crazy. She hits on me all the damned time. What about you, Lucas?"

Lucas shook his head. "Nope. She never has."

Mitch howled, "I don't believe that shit! She used to rub herself all over Gunner when he was here. The girl is hot to trot."

"I thought guys preferred girls like her?" I directed my question to Lucas in particular.

He joked. "Maybe she isn't into Indians?"

Mitch was quiet for a moment, then broke into laughter. "She's not the picky kind, Lucas. I've heard too much. But, hey, if you want me to hook you up…"

Lucas shook his head. "No thanks. She's not my type either."

Valerie peeped through the screen door.

"Mitch, are you ready to go?"

"Yeah, baby." he called out. He reached to shake Lucas's hand. "Congrats again, brother. Sorry to run out on our graduation party, but I have a hot date."

After they drove away, Lucas sat in the chair beside me. With my cousin out of sight, I was more at ease. "So, tell me, what is your type?"

"I don't know, maybe a girl that's a little more wholesome."

"I don't know too many of those around here." I teased.

"Nope." He leaned back and looked up at the darkening sky. "I heard that people in big cities can't see the stars, with all the bright lights and all. That must be sad."

While he continued to study the sky, I studied him. It was the first time I realized that he was now a grown man. Something unusual stirred deep within my stomach. It was weird and pleasant, and all at the same time.

"Look!" He pointed.

Caught up in my thoughts, I jumped, and barely caught a glimpse of the shooting star.

"Did you make a wish?" I asked.

His eyes met mine. "Yeah, but that wish will be on hold for a while. I'm leaving for Wyoming in a few days. I took a job up there, so I guess you won't see me until the holidays."

I resisted a frown and pretended to be happy for him. It's not like Lucas was a prospect for me. He was way too close, like family. Besides, dating was yet to be cleared by my Daddy, who seemed to be dragging his feet on the subject.

"Gosh, things are going to be different with both you and Gunner away," I said. "We'll have to stay in touch, though."

After a few moments of silence, he responded. "Is it okay if I call you?"

"Yes, I'd like that."

Two days later, Aunt Katie and Uncle Stan received a call from Gunner's staff sergeant. He explained that their unit had been involved in an ambush, and Gunner was hit twice. After rescue, Gunner was taken to a field hospital, and still in surgery at the time of the call. No additional information was given, but they were promised an update when possible.

After twenty-four terrifying hours, my aunt and uncle received more details. Gunner took two shots; one in the chest and the other to his lower left leg. Fortunately, he didn't have to wait long for rescue, and a helicopter crew arrived to fly him and a comrade away. Gunner's injuries required surgery, which he had come through successfully, and his condition was listed as stable.

A few days later, Gunner was able to call home. He reported that the doctors expected a full recovery, other than a possible limp. He told Uncle Stan that his friends on the helicopter crew were checking on him regularly.

Gunner also mentioned that since his tour of duty was near completion, he would be coming home after recovery.

Relieved and thankful, our family came together to plan his homecoming party. "The horses and I will be here," Uncle Ted pledged. "Put me down for steaks and beer." I offered to decorate. As Mom and Aunt Katie discussed the menu, Grandma interrupted them. "He'll want my potato salad."

"Save something on your list for me and Val," Mitch said. "We'll help, too."

Gillie and I celebrated the last week of our sophomore year at the Main Street Pharmacy. We ordered cherry Cokes, and grabbed a booth to sit and conjure up some summer fun. As I listened to her nonstop chattering, I caught a glimpse of the new pharmacist. He noticed, and then quickly looked away. Gillie whirled around to see.

"What did I miss?"

"He must be the new pharmacist," I said. "I guess Sam Higgins finally retired."

"And he's good-looking, ooh la la." Gillie said before turning back around in her seat. "Sam creeped me out with all that heavy breathing. And when he talked, his nose whistled."

Moments later, the new pharmacist walked toward us. He appeared neat and clean-cut in his starched lab coat. I was already impressed. He stopped, and rapped a knuckle on our table. "Hi girls, or ladies that is. Ready for some refills?"

We looked down at our half-full glasses. "Not yet, but thanks." Gillie told him.

He never even looked at her, but trained his eyes on me.

"I'm Steven Fitzgerald," he said. "By chance, are either of you interested in a summer job? I'd like to hire a part-time assistant."

Up to this point, I had not spoken, but decided to put my well-taught courtesy to use. "Nice to meet you, Steven. I'm Sara, and this is my friend, Gillie." Gillie's eyes widened as I continued. "Yes, I might be interested, but I have no job experience."

Gillie glared at me.

Steven nodded. "That's quite all right. I'm willing to train my new hire. How 'bout I grab an application? Be right back." He disappeared behind the counter.

Gillie couldn't contain herself. "Oh my God! You seriously want to work here?"

"I don't know yet, it depends. I need to talk to my parents first. I wonder if he gives discounts to the employees?"

"You don't take drugs." she scolded.

"No, but think of the makeup and perfume I can save on."

Steven returned. "Get this back to me soon, okay? It was nice meeting you both."

He turned his back to Gillie, winked covertly at me, then went back to work.

I shoved the application in my purse and immediately changed the subject. "Gillie, you have to come to Gunner's homecoming party. Everyone's going to be there."

She scoffed, crossed her arms and scooted back in her seat. "Gee, I sure hope you don't have to work that day."

I received my last letter from Vietnam just days before Gunner's discharge from the Army. He'd grown bored during the lengthy hospitalization, and his letters were longer and more detailed. I saved all of them, and kept them in a pretty box on my dresser. The box once served as Grandma's recipe holder; its wooden lid was carved with assorted herbs. I sprinkled homemade potpourri in the bottom, made with ingredients that she and I gathered on a hike: cedar chips, blackberry leaves, honeysuckle and rosemary. I also threw in a cone of strawberry-scented incense.

I re-read Gunner's letter a couple of times. He was on the mend and looked forward to coming home again. His thoughts on the war had changed since he left here, and he struggled with the reasons our country ever got involved. He wrote about the wounded soldiers around him, their conversations and poker games. Most of what he divulged to me was fairly pleasant. He kept the horrors to himself, which was his nature.

Gunner mentioned his gratitude to Lance Ferguson, and described him as "a good friend and a patriot...But maybe a little shady." He signed off with, "I'll see you very soon. Love – Gunner."

On the morning of Gunner's return, Uncle Stan and Aunt Katie drove to Tulsa to pick him up at the airport. I could hardly wait to see him. Mom and I arrived early to Grandma's house and went straight to work. I grabbed a ladder and hung a "WELCOME HOME" banner across the top of the porch. Mitch crept up behind me. "It looks crooked," he joked.

"So's your head," I said.

Uncle Ted arrived with Spirit, Lady, and Aspen. Mitch hurried to greet them. After clearing it with Grandma, Ted set up his "bar" on the pickup's tailgate. Beer was iced down in galvanized buckets, and a few bottles of whiskey were set out. My dad soon arrived, and joined Uncle Ted for a beer, then they prepared to grill the steaks.

Grandma's rose bushes were in full bloom. A lazy wind blew from the south, whipping the tall grass out in the field. The Mimosa tree in the corner of the yard swayed, and strew its feathery pink blossoms about the lawn.

We placed box fans throughout the house to keep everyone comfortable. After Grandma Janie set the table, she lined the countertops with fresh steaming vegetables, homemade yeast rolls, and desserts.

Mom announced, "They should be here any minute."

We cheered as the car appeared, with Uncle Stan behind the wheel. Tears of joy fell as we caught first sight of

Gunner in the passenger seat. As soon as the car came to a stop, Gunner stepped out and grabbed his crutches. He immediately reached for Grandma Janie, and hugged her for the longest time. After she released him, she stepped back, looked him up and down, and smiled.

"My, my…You're way too thin. But I have just the remedy for that."

He laughed and greeted the others. Going down the line, he finally made his way to me. He seemed taken aback at first, studying my blue halter top and cut-off denim shorts.

"Oh, my Lord! You've grown up, Sara. Was I really gone for that long?"

Mitch interrupted, placing a bottle of Jack Daniels in Gunner's hand. "I heard she has two, maybe three boy-friends."

I rolled my eyes. "Lies!"

Gunner leaned against a fence post and scanned the yard. "Where's Lucas?

Mitch filled him in. "He's still in Wyoming. He'll probably come around soon."

Gunner pressed the bottle to his lips. "I'd like to see Wyoming someday."

After a couple of sips, he passed the bottle back. "Right now, I'm lucky to be in Oklahoma, much less breathing."

Mitch wiped his mouth after a long pull on the bottle. "Yeah, thanks to those buddies of yours."

"The Bayou Bad Asses saved my life for sure. I only remember bits and pieces, but the medics slung me on that chopper in a dead run. When Lance saw it was me, he said, *"We gotcha, Pardner."* As we lifted off, he yelled, *"Move over you motherfuckers, we're comin' through!"* I was in so much pain, I wasn't sure I'd make it. And if that wasn't bad enough, we started taking on fire. Dodging artillery is much scarier in the sky than on the ground. Lance was slinging us all over the back of that Huey, but he got us out of there."

Mitch nodded. "I'd like to shake his hand someday. Hey, when you're healed up, let me know if you want a job. I can probably get you on at the mill."

Gunner took the bottle back from Mitch. "Yeah? I should be off these crutches in a few weeks."

Mitch was quick to begin the ribbing. "I'd be glad to train you. It'll be like old times, like when I taught you how to ride a horse. And to shoot. And to pick up girls…"

Gunner didn't miss a beat. "My ass you did."

The conversation was broken up by Uncle Ted's curses. With a Lone Star beer in one hand, he swung a spatula with the other.

My dad sprung toward him. "Need some help, Ted?"

"Hell yes, somebody needs to come swat at these god-damned flies.'

Mitch gestured at our uncle. "Gunner, you might be the hero, but I aim to be just like him when I get old."

Gunner chuckled. "Yeah, well I'm afraid they broke the mold after he was born. By the way, where's this Valerie I've been hearing so much about?"

Mitch raised his brows. "She'll be here soon. I'll introduce you, but don't be flirting with my woman."

Gunner laughed and wagged a finger. "I hear she's hot, so don't stray too far. How serious is this deal?"

"We're about to move in together. Found a house just the other day."

"I'd say that's pretty serious," Gunner said. "I'm happy for you, especially considering she's taking you off the market. Opens it wide up for me." He patted Mitch's back and laughed. "Excuse me, but I have a few more hellos to say."

He walked towards Spirit, Lady, and Aspen, who waited patiently.

Indian Summer came and went. Blue skies gave way to gray. Maples, pin oaks and sweet gums were flaming with the colors of fall. Acorns scattered the ground; the nights were long and cool. Things were back to normal, which especially pleased Grandma Janie. Her house was the place to be again, and the designated scene for Uncle Ted's Friday night poker games.

Other than my cousins, Dad and Uncle Stan sometimes joined in the games. Grandma tidied up the house and prepared homemade treats for them. Sometimes, if I didn't have other plans, I offered to come and help her.

One night, Uncle Ted burst through the front door with a twelve-pack under his arm. He stopped short of the kitchen and greeted Grandma, who was kicked back in her easy chair. "*Osiyo,*" he said; "Hello" in Cherokee.

Grandma smiled. "Hello, my brother. Mitch and Gunner are waiting in the kitchen."

"I'm running a little late. Had to make a stop at the store." He proceeded to make his case. "Now Janie, I know the house rules, but it's a little too nippy to drink this beer outside. Just this once, will you pardon us?"

A little skeptical, she nodded and waved him on through. "Just as long as you don't make a habit of it. And don't get too rowdy in there."

"No danger in that, considering we only get 4 apiece."

She snickered as he passed through.

Ted stepped into the kitchen, took 3 beers from the carton and handed a couple to Mitch and Gunner. He seated himself at the table and dealt the cards. Soon, laughter spilled from the kitchen, and the bullshit got deeper by the minute. They kept their jokes semi-clean, out of respect for me and Grandma. Every now and then, Grandma adjusted the tv volume to drown out their noise. After she nodded off, I went to see who was winning. As usual, it was Gunner, who seemed to have sharpened his skills during the hospital stay. "Wanna' play with us, Sara?" he offered. "I'll teach you."

"I'll just watch for now," I said. "Maybe next time." I was expecting a call from Gillie anyway.

"You don't want to learn from either of these two, believe me," Uncle Ted joked. "How's the part-time job going, sis?" He often called me "sis," rather than Sara.

"It's good. I like it so far. I'm saving for a car."

He thought for a moment. "My neighbor has a 1970 Jeep for sale. He took good care of it too. You and your daddy should go look at it."

I shrugged. "A Jeep? I guess that's pretty cool. What color is it?"

Uncle Ted chuckled. "It's red, sis. Don't worry, you'll look great in it." he lowered his voice. "I'm not trying to alarm you, but just let me know if that pharmacist does anything to make you uncomfortable, okay?" He peered over his reading glasses and waited for my reply. My face went hot with embarrassment. What was he getting at? I suddenly felt like a deer in headlights.

"Um, yeah, I will."

Gunner and Mitch turned in their chairs. Oh God, why did Uncle Ted have to say it in front of them? He gave them a perfect excuse to butt in. I bolted down the hallway, and stepped into the bathroom. Once inside, I cracked the door to listen.

Mitch began the interrogation. "What do you know about that guy?"

Uncle Ted didn't answer, but studied his cards intently.

"You must know something?" Gunner added.

Ted tried to downplay the situation. "No facts, only rumors."

As usual, Mitch grew hotter. "If he thinks he'll get away with…"

Uncle Ted must have cut him a look, because Mitch didn't say anything else.

Throughout my school years, I was less than appreciative of the male members of our family. Their over-protectiveness could be totally embarrassing. Like the time Mitch punched my classmate Charlie Dean in the nose after Charlie stuck a foot out to trip me. Poor Charlie made the mistake of swinging back at Mitch, and soon found himself on the ground. Mitch stood over him for a moment, but didn't say a word. Charlie got the message. I watched anxiously and feared the worst. Much to my surprise, Mitch extended a hand to help Charlie up.

I scolded Mitch on the bus ride home that day, and asked why he had to make such a scene. "That's my job," he explained. "Best get used to it." Gunner, who had missed the fiasco, was so amused with the story that he asked to hear it a second time.

I hadn't given much thought to Uncle Ted's comment, until the following week at work, when I noticed Steven's lingering gazes. As I took a break one day, he came over and sat at my booth. He made small talk while I sipped my milkshake, and asked about my grades and ambitions. I told him I was considering a career in the medical field.

"I believe medicine is a great choice for you," he said. "It's obvious that you care about our customers, and they think highly of you. If you need any advice, just let me know. I'm always here for you."

His blue eyes sparkled as he stood and straightened his lab coat. I watched him walk away, then he turned and caught me in the act. Whether I wanted to admit it or not, there was an undeniable chemistry between us.

Later, I had my nightly phone chat with Gillie. "I hear music," she said. "Who are you listening to right now?"

"Elton John. What about you?" I asked, though I was more interested in the business section of our local newspaper. It displayed a picture of Steven, arms crossed and smiling, in front of the pharmacy.

"I Don't Need No Doctor." She sighed. "I'm really getting into Humble Pie, and I love Peter Frampton. I think I want to marry him."

I yawned and stretched out on my bed. "Mmm, yeah he's foxy. Oh! Did I tell you that Mitch and Valerie found a cute little house? They've already moved in together and are planning their wedding."

"Wow," she gushed. "That's so cool. What are you going to wear? Make sure to ask for that day off from work. And how's your job going? Does Mr. Fitzgerald flirt with you?" Gillie was on a roll.

"Steven is very nice. I like him."

"Oh, so it's Steven now? Sounds like you've become friends already."

I attempted to save face. "No, I didn't mean it like that."

"Sara, tell me the truth…Are you attracted to him?"

My cheeks tingled, and though I wanted to lie, I couldn't. "Well, I think he's handsome, if that's what you mean?"

Her voice became serious. "As long as you keep his wedding ring in mind, it's acceptable to find him handsome. Don't quote me though; you probably won't find that printed in the Bible."

I became quiet. A pang of guilt, maybe?

Gillie's voice broke the silence. "Sara?"

"Yeah?" I whispered.

"Just be careful."

I turned defensive. "What are you talking about, Gillie? He's not that kind of a guy. He's a professional."

"Don't get all upset," she laughed. "Has he tried to kiss you?"

"No, I told you it's not like that. You're acting like my cousins."

"Come on, you know you can trust me. I'm not anything like Mitch and Gunner. Remember when we were in eighth grade and they told on us for skipping class?" Gillie knew how to make me laugh. "And what about the time we hitchhiked home from the store?"

My anger cooled. "Boy, did I get in big trouble over that. We'll never get away with anything as long as my cousins are around, it's like they have eyes in the back of their heads."

Gillie agreed. "And I'll never hitchhike again as long as I live. Gunner put the fear of God in me. Remember all the scary stuff he and Mitch warned us about? Like axe murderers?"

I giggled. "Oh Gillie, don't be ridiculous. It was the preacher's son who gave us a ride that day."

"In Paulette's opinion, preacher's sons are the worst and should be avoided at all costs."

"I'm guessing she knows this from experience, right?"

We laughed out loud. I tried to cover my tracks before we said good night. "Please don't tell anyone about my friendship with Steven. There's really nothing to it anyway."

I tried to fall asleep, but found myself wondering what it would be like to kiss Steven. Though I fantasized about his touch, he could never know. I would keep my desires completely to myself.

On a Saturday morning in mid-November, I sprang out of bed, giddy with the excitement of Mitch and Valerie's wedding. My fancy new dress hung before me. I admired the sparkly platform shoes I found to match it. There was a light rap on my bedroom door. "Sara?" my dad called.

Surprised, I opened the door. Most weekends, he was out early to begin his work around the property.

"Get dressed and come outside. The wind felled some limbs last night, and I need your help."

I closed the door and sighed, nonplussed with the thought of chores this early. But at least I'd have them out of the way. After I dressed myself in jeans, a flannel shirt and my old Justin ropers, I bailed out the front door. To my surprise, a red Jeep sat in the driveway. Momma stood by the driver's door. Daddy walked up the path to meet me, dangling the keys and smiling from ear to ear.

My eyes grew wide. "It's mine?" I cried.

"Yes," Dad replied. "Well, after you learn to drive a stick to my satisfaction, that is."

Standard transmission or not, I had my very own vehicle, and suddenly all was well in the universe.

Though pained to leave my Jeep at home, I rode with my parents to church that evening. As we entered the double doors, the scene was nothing short of magical. I stopped in my tracks, because the church seemed like the setting of a fairytale. The only light came from the candles. As the flames flickered, their reflections danced back and forth on the stained-glass windows.

We seated ourselves in the front pew with the rest of our family. I took my place next to Grandma Janie. When the music began, Valerie seemed to float all the way down the aisle, escorted by her father. Mitch smiled proudly as she approached.

Gunner and Lucas were by his side. They all wore tuxedos and stood with shoulders back, hands crossed in front. The whole scene made my heart happy. I nudged Grandma and nodded toward the guys. When Lucas caught our stares, his lips curved into a bashful grin.

The vows were simple and heartfelt. Then Mitch pulled his new bride close and kissed her sweetly. Soon after, he whisked her back down the aisle through a flurry of pink flower petals. We met them at the reception, held in the private dining room of Mitch's favorite restaurant, Big Tex's Roadhouse. My parents shared a table with Uncle

Stan and Aunt Katie. I headed for Gillie and Paulette's table. The way Paulette eyed Mitch and Valerie didn't give me the impression she was happy for them. "I hope Valerie takes good care of him," she said, "because there's plenty of other girls around here who..."

I intentionally cut her off. "She's perfect for him. They'll be just fine together."

Paulette shrugged. "Yeah, I guess."

After Paulette and Gillie left, I wound my way around to locate Grandma and Uncle Ted. Familiar laughter filled the air, it was coming from my parents' table. Momma and Aunt Katie sported matching beehive hairdo's and bright-colored nail polish. They giggled together, no doubt at one of Uncle Stan's inappropriate jokes.

Grandma admired the newlyweds as they mingled with their guests. "This is the happiest I've ever seen Mitch." she said.

"Yep, I agree." Uncle Ted replied.

He scanned the room. "Say, where did Lucas run off to? Do either of you know how long he'll be in town?"

"He'll be here until after Thanksgiving," I said.

Grandma Janie touched my hand. "You should invite him over to our table. He likes you. Always has."

"I hope you're not suggesting I date Lucas?" I argued. "He's like family."

"Hell, is that so bad?" my uncle said.

I shook my head in disbelief. Lucas stood at the bar, so I waved my hand to catch his attention. He brought his beer over and pulled out a chair.

I checked him out while he visited with us. No doubt I was attracted to him, but why risk messing up a good friendship? Besides, he regarded me as a kid sister.

When my parents were ready to leave, I asked permission to stay longer, and told them I would find a ride home. Lucas and I joined the wedding table, where Gunner had everyone's attention. He told us about experiences in faraway places. A beautiful brunette was glued to his side. He looked relaxed and confident, and well-adjusted to civilian life.

Months earlier, Gunner had taken Mitch's lead, and accepted a job at the mill. He'd volunteered to work as many overtime hours as possible, and it paid off. He bought a Firebird Trans Am, and soon after, found a house to rent. The job also served as a distraction from his memories of the war.

I asked Lucas for a ride home that night. During the drive, he told me about life in Wyoming, and how the brutal weather had slowed most construction work. He described the large ranches and the beautiful mountains there. All too soon, we pulled into my driveway.

Lucas stopped and shifted the truck into park. He nervously tapped on the steering wheel.

"I'm really happy for Mitch. Valerie seems like a great girl."

I raised an eyebrow and teased him. "Could be you next."

He shot me a suspicious look. "Huh?"

"Walking down the aisle. Maybe you'll be next."

He snickered. "Nah, not any time soon for me."

I touched his arm. "More likely you than Gunner. Variety is the spice of his life."

Lucas studied my hand on his arm, then broke into a wide smile. "Mitch and I call him 'The Playboy.'"

We laughed together. I thought about my earlier conversation with Grandma and Uncle Ted, and considered telling Lucas about it. But at the last minute, I changed my mind. Maybe another day.

After Mitch and Valerie's wedding, the holidays kind of sneaked up on us. It was a Friday night, when I had decided to sleep over at Grandma's house. I stretched the phone cord to the front porch swing for a chat with Gillie, when Mitch and Valerie drove up. Gunner was right behind them in his car. Mitch parked, walked around to the back of his truck, and pulled the tailgate down. He and Gunner unloaded a beautiful new dining room set, an early Christmas gift for Grandma Janie. I told Gillie I'd call her back, and went to help my cousins. The three of them had put their money together to buy the furniture. Grandma was very surprised, and dabbed the stray tears as they fell on her cheeks. Mitch and Valerie set the furniture to her liking, then hugged her and went home. Gunner stuck around. He sat on the sofa and patted the cushion next to him. "Come talk with me, Grandma. I want to run something by you."

She sat, and gave him her full attention. I picked up a fashion magazine and went to the kitchen, but within ear range.

"Do you remember when I wrote to you about Lance Ferguson?" he asked.

"Yes, the young man from Hot Springs," Grandma said.

"That's right. Well, he's home and I went to see him the other day. He wants to go into business together."

Grandma's voice seemed puzzled. "What? You mean you'd have to leave your good job at the mill? I thought you were happy there?"

"No, no. Not at first. Actually, it depends on the success of the business. I'll be working there in the evenings, after my shift at the mill." he explained.

Grandma cut right to the chase. "What kind of business?"

He hesitated for a moment, then laid out his plans. "With Waya being such a small town, we only have a few restaurants to choose from. Lance would like to buy a few acres of land and build a bar & grill. A nice place to hang out, and shoot some pool, with a good menu."

I peeped around the doorway. Grandma's back stiffened, "And liquor?"

Gunner patted her hands as if he had expected this reaction.

"Grandma, I know how you feel about alcohol, and I totally get it. But there's not much to do around here, you know? Lance grew up in the restaurant business. He learned a lot from his parents, and he's prepared to finance the place. Since he lives in Arkansas, he wants me to manage it. I have a lot of great ideas for this."

Grandma studied his face. "I'm curious. Why here? Has Lance ever been to Waya?"

"No, not yet," Gunner said. "Soon, though."

"I don't mean to sound negative; I just find it strange that Lance would want to invest in a town he's never set foot in. Why not build his bar in Hot Springs? It's a tourist town. Doesn't this strike you as being odd?" Grandma said.

Gunner hesitated. "Maybe it's because of everything I've told him about my home town, and he really believes our business will add to its charm."

"I appreciate your honesty," Grandma said, "and I wish you luck with this venture. A café or restaurant is perfectly fine, and it's true that we could use a few more here. But, just a word of warning, any establishment that resembles a honky-tonk usually takes on a bad reputation fast."

She stood and motioned him to follow her into the kitchen. I stared down at my magazine innocently. She reached for a dust rag, and ran it across her new table. "What do you plan to name this bar and grill?"

"The Foxhole," he answered.

She studied him. "And what does Mitch think?"

"He agreed that it'll be good for our town. Hopefully he'll help me get it started up. I'm sure he'd make a good bouncer."

Grandma objected. "Please put someone else in that position. Someone with an even temper."

I didn't have an opinion of The Foxhole, but it quickly became a sore subject in our family. Grandma, Mom and Aunt Katie were against the idea. But the plans were moving right along. Lance purchased land that sat conveniently near the state highway running through, and a ground-breaking ceremony was scheduled. Gunner was as busy as a dog chasing its tail. A perfectionist, he worried excessively over every small detail.

I stopped by his house to visit one day. He was lounging on the sofa. Stacks of paperwork were on the coffee table. He smiled a lot, and was excited to share details of the bar's construction. "It's going to be nice," he told me, "Not at all like a honky-tonk. Just wait 'til you see the menu."

"I hope you can pull it off, but you've sure got everyone all worked up." I teased.

"I know." He shook his head. "Maybe they'll settle down soon. It's not like I don't appreciate my job at the mill, but it's not where I want to be for the rest of my life. Vietnam taught me a few things. I did my duty and I survived it. Don't I deserve this opportunity? I realize it'll be a whole new ballgame for me, but I want to make it a success. And hopefully I can count on Mitch to have my back."

I squinted. "With what? Flipping burgers?"

"Wherever I need him…An occasional bartender, or security."

"I'm not so sure Valerie will go for that. They're still newlyweds. I wouldn't want my husband working at a bar."

"Come on, she can trust him. He's not the type to chase skirts."

"It's the skirts that worry me," I said.

Gunner sighed. "Where's the faith, cuz? You're starting to sound like the others."

I suddenly realized he was right. "I'm sorry. I didn't come here to discourage you. I'm excited for you, Gunner. And I understand you want to make a good change in our town." I scooted closer to him. "Know what? The Foxhole might be the perfect place to celebrate my eighteenth birthday."

"Damn, I don't think I'm ready for it. Our little Sara is about to be legal."

I hugged him, then stood to leave. "Keep me posted on your progress, okay?"

He winked and gave me a thumbs-up

The Foxhole opened for business in the first week of May. Mitch accepted Gunner's job offer, promising Valerie it was only temporary. A few weeks later, Gillie and I graduated from high school. My entire family attended the ceremony, and friends, too. Except for Lucas, who couldn't get off work for the trip.

Afterward, Gillie and I met up with our classmates at a honky-tonk. On a dare, I rode the mechanical bull, which threw me off in four seconds. Then it was Gillie's turn. She lasted eight seconds on the ride, but busted out the seam of her jeans in the process, exposing her bright pink panties. I took off my jacket and wrapped it around her. We laughed as we ran across the parking lot to my Jeep.

We weren't ready for the night to end, so I chose to take the backroads home. We didn't discuss anything serious along the way, but we knew big changes were coming. Gillie was actively looking for a job. I planned to work full-time at the pharmacy, and was enrolled in general classes at our community college.

With my increased interest in medicine, I consulted with Grandma Janie, who promised to teach me her native remedies. We went for outings around her land, just like we did when I was a child. We gathered herbs and foraged for roots. Some for drying, others for soaking. We made teas and poultices, ointments and elixirs. Grandma taught me everything she had learned from the Red Eagle side of the family; how to handle plants with caution, their benefits, as well as their dangers. I learned the recipes and recorded them on paper, then tucked them away in the wooden box on my dresser.

On July Fourth, 1975, our family gathered at a place known as "the crossing," an area of the Illinois River shallow enough to cross in a pickup. We sat up our picnic tables on the flat banks. Uncle Ted brought a barbeque grill. Everyone was there, except for Valerie. When I asked Mitch about it, he quickly brushed me off. But I pressed on him until he gave in. He admitted that they had fought earlier. "She'll get over it, though." he said.

"How disrespectful of you." I scolded.

He gave me that look, the one that always went right through me. He jumped to defend himself. "She knows I'm only working at The Foxhole temporarily. Why is it such a big deal if I stay for a few beers after closing? She's always asleep when I got home, for crying out loud."

I took the opportunity to bust his chops. "Typical excuse."

Gunner came toward us. Mitch took a big swig of beer and pointed at me. "Watch it, Gunner. This one's feeling scrappy today."

Gunner stopped and held up both hands. "Don't shoot."

"I'm trying to teach him some manners," I said.

Gunner laughed. "Sara, does Mitch have your permission to go fishing with me tonight? Uncle Ted said we can use his Jon boat. I smell a fish fry coming up."

Mitch nodded. "Hell yeah. Lucas is on his way right now. We'll take him with us."

I cleared my throat. "Mitch, aren't you forgetting something?"

He threw the empty beer can in his truck bed. "Like what?"

I put my hands on my hips. "Like discussing this fishing trip with your wife first?"

"Holy shit, why do I tell you my business? You'll hold it over my head for the rest of my life."

Gunner took a step back. "Look, I don't want to come between you and Val. Just let me know later."

Mitch shook his head. "No man, it's cool."

I glared at him. No doubt he got the message.

The following day, Grandma and I got a good laugh when Uncle Ted told us about the fishing trip.

"I hope y'all didn't have your hopes up for a fish fry," he said.

"Uh oh…What happened last night?" Grandma asked.

"I got the story when they brought my boat home earlier. Around 2 am, the fishing was just gettin' good when Lucas reached for his beer and came face to face with a big ole' cottonmouth. I guess the snake had slithered in unnoticed and wanted in on the fishing party. Lucas let out a yelp, and damned near pissed himself. That didn't set well with the snake, because it coiled up and got ready to brawl. So, while Lucas held the lantern, Mitch and Gunner looked for something to whack the snake with. The snake struck at Lucas and when he jumped out of its reach, he bumped into Gunner, who almost fell overboard."

Uncle Ted slapped his knee and laughed until his face turned red. We were anxious to hear the rest, but had to wait for him to catch his breath.

"Mitch had a pistol, but was afraid he'd shoot a hole in the bottom of the boat. So, the snake started to make itself at home, and crawled around the boat. The boys were getting all tripped up, trying to stay out of its path. The boat was rocking back and forth, and needless to say, it almost flipped over. So, the three of them had to bail out and swim to shore. When they went back to recover my boat this morning, no snake. I guess it had moved on to bigger adventures.”

“Well, that explains why Gunner came by for my turnip root ointment. He must've gotten into some poison oak.” Grandma said.

Uncle Ted nodded. “Well, that's a story for their grandkids someday. You should have seen their faces when I teased them about letting a little ole' snake ruin the whole night. Amateurs.”

“Did they say how big the cottonmouth was?” I asked.

“Oh, five feet long, give or take.”

My jaw dropped. “Oh my God!”

“I believe I would have bailed out, too.” Grandma said.

A few weeks later, Paulette drove me and Gillie to Tulsa for our first live concert. We checked into the hotel, then headed to the venue where the rock group, Heart was to perform. Gillie and I were beyond excited. When the show started, we jumped to our feet and danced until the very end. Ann and Nancy Wilson, in their true, rock 'n' roll badass style, made a great impression on me. I left that night with a sense of female empowerment that I wanted to feel forever.

Paulette suggested a Mexican restaurant for dinner. “We passed one a few miles back. Let's go.” After enchiladas and margaritas, we walked to a nearby country bar. The moment we stepped inside its doors, we attracted hungry stares from the cowboys seated at the bar.

"BINGO!" Paulette said. "I don't know about you two, but I might get lucky tonight."

Gillie and I exchanged worried looks. "You better not abandon us, Paulette," Gillie said. "We don't know our way around this huge city."

"Why are you being such babies? We're here to celebrate you're eighteenth birthdays, so don't go cramping my style."

I elbowed Gillian. "Let's hope she doesn't pick up an axe murderer, Gillie. I hear about them on the news all the time."

Paulette wasn't amused. "Let's try to have some fun, you losers."

We found an empty table and were soon approached by several pairs of boots. Beers were coming to us from all around. Gillie and I were shy about dancing, but Paulette hit the floor like a dancehall queen. "Let her do her thing," I persuaded Gillie. "After all, she drove us up here."

I scanned the room, and the crowd seemed much older than us.

"Have you ever danced with a guy?" Gillie asked.

"Just my cousins. Oh, and there was that time when Uncle Ted taught me the Two-Step. I've already forgotten it, though."

Gillie closed her eyes and blinked repeatedly. "The cigarette smoke is making my eyes burn. Wanna' walk outside for a bit?"

We informed Paulette, then made our way through the mass. Once outside, we walked to a spot under a flashing neon sign.

"Are you having a good time?" I asked.

"Yeah, I mean, I'm not really used to these places. My sister is in her element, though."

"It's a nice change of scenery," I said. "Even if it's only a couple of days."

A lone cowboy ambled up the sidewalk. He did a double take when he noticed us. "Morning ladies! Wait a minute…This ain't morning. Your smiles are so purdy and bright, I got a little confused."

We laughed. He whirled to look over his shoulder. "Lee! You comin'?" he yelled. "There's some girls over here as fine as frog hair."

He removed his hat. "Forgive my lack of manners. I'm Billy Jack."

His comrade stepped from the darkness. He wore a black Stetson, Wrangler jeans, and a grin as wide as the Mississippi. Billy Jack motioned him over. "Ladies, meet my cousin Lee. He's being just a little bashful tonight."

Gillie and I introduced ourselves. After a bit of small talk, we agreed to go inside with Billy Jack and Lee. Paulette never noticed. She was hot on the dance floor; a different partner with each new song. While Billy Jack showed Gillie his dance moves, Lee and I had a chance to make a connection. He was a little awkward, and less out-going than his cousin, but I found him easy to talk to. His good manners impressed me.

Come to find out, Lee was two years older than me, and worked at an auto parts store in his home town. We lived only 30 miles apart. I also learned that he was an amateur calf roper with hopes of entering the rodeo cir-cuit. By last call, he had loosened up and began to flirt with me. By closing time, he'd worked up enough nerve to ask for my phone number.

"Did you get lucky, Sara?" Paulette asked after we re-turned to our hotel room.

"What do you mean?"

"I saw you and your cutie pie walk outside once."

"Actually, that's when he asked for my phone num-ber." I informed her.

Gillie rolled her eyes. "Do you honestly think she's that easy, Paulette?"

"Poor guy! You could've at least given him a bj." Pau-lette teased.

"Oh my God!" I exclaimed.

"Paulette, for crying out loud..." Gillie scoffed.

"Can you prudes take a joke? You're grownups, for God's sake. Say goodbye to your Sunday school vocabu-laries. It's over now."

"Doesn't mean we have to speak in your barfly lan-guage." Gillie fired back.

Our weekend in the city passed by too quickly. After a movie and some shopping on Sunday, we headed back to Waya. I had only been home for a couple of hours when Lee called me for the first time.

Come Monday, I was on Cloud Nine. Lee and I had a date planned for the upcoming weekend. At work, I day-dreamed as I stocked the toiletry aisle. Steven walked up from behind and called my name.

He motioned me to the breakroom. "Sara? Got a minute?"

I followed him, a little baffled with his request.

"Would you be able to stay a while after closing?" He asked.

I nodded. "Sure, what can I help with?"

"I'm a little down," he answered. "Maybe if I talk about it to someone, I can put things into perspective. Know what I mean?"

"Of course."

I'm sure my expression showed genuine concern, but my gut was suspicious. Still, I gave Steven the benefit of the doubt. After my co-worker, Lori left for the day, Steven closed up and locked the doors. We sat together in the breakroom, and I listened as he poured out his heart. He talked about his issues, mostly marriage-related, and complained about his overbearing wife, Janet.

He explained that they married right out of college, and though he wanted to wait, she pressured him to start a family. He soon found out how relentless she could be, and in order to keep the peace, he gave in. After the births of their two children, Janet developed an obsession with keeping up with the Jones's. Her luxuries had exceeded his income, which pushed them into great debt. When I asked if he'd tried to reason with her, he said he had on many occasions. In his opinion, their relationship was over and he wanted a divorce.

Being inexperienced with such things, the only advice I could suggest was counseling and patience. "It's worth a shot, if you still love her?" I asked.

"I'm not sure," he said, "Sometimes I wonder if anyone would even date me again?"

A baited question, maybe? But I encouraged him to stay positive.

"Just keep your chin up, Steven. I'm sure there must be a solution to save your marriage."

Lee and I spent the next few months getting to know each other. We usually went out on Friday and Saturday nights. Sometimes we met halfway between our home towns, but one particular night, he picked me up at home. He seemed eager to chat with my parents, and was in no hurry to leave. I could tell that they were as impressed with his manners as I was.

We said goodbye and he drove me to a drive-in theater. We stood in line for hot dogs, sodas, and popcorn, then carried it all to his pickup. Every now and then, he leaned over for a kiss. Near the end of the film, it started raining.

Vehicles around us trickled away, but we stayed put. "It'll probably stop soon." Lee said.

He pulled me closer, and we scooted down in the seat. One kiss led to another, each more passionate than the last. He didn't seem nervous at all, which gave me the indication he might be experienced. With the windows completely fogged, and the rain thumping the roof of his pickup, we went all the way. My first experience, awkward and brief, wasn't as great as I'd imagined it would be. Despite the letdown, I couldn't wait to share my news with Gillie.

The more involved Lee and I became, the more obsessive Steven got. It's like he sensed something was different about me. Every Monday, he pressed for details on my weekend activities. He also took a greater interest in my clothing choices, and complimented me when I wore something new. If nobody was around, he whistled softly as I walked by.

My curves developed, especially my bust line, as I blossomed into a young woman. Ample cleavage, a common trait in the women of our family, had not skipped me. Gillie said she would kill for my boobs, but they made me feel self-conscious.

She advised, "Sara, you should flaunt what the Lord gave you."

Gillie and I loved makeup, and spent hours applying it on each other. I could paint on liquid eyeliner like a pro. Now that I was over eighteen, I took chances with deeper shades of lipstick, instead of my usual pale pink. Steven took notice when I shopped the cosmetics aisle, often begging me to model lipsticks for him. He asked to watch as I applied them, and he especially liked the red shades. He encouraged me to wear them at work. At first, I didn't see any harm in his requests, but it eventually started to creep me out. Now that I was going steady with Lee, my little crush on Steven had fallen by the wayside.

In my eyes, Lee and I had reached a new relationship level, so it was time that he met the rest of my family…Gunner and Mitch included. Though the idea made me a little nervous, I had a plan. I showed up at their weekly poker game and strolled into the kitchen. After I circled the table, I seated myself, and pretended to be interested in the game.

"Friday night and no hot date?" Gunner teased. "You might as well start playing cards with us."

"My boyfriend, Lee, is busy tonight. He's practicing at a friend's corral."

"Practicing?" Uncle Ted asked.

"He wants to make it into the rodeo circuit." I replied.

Mitch joshed me. "As a barrel racer?"

Uncle Ted almost choked on a pretzel, while Gunner tried to hold his laugh. Things weren't going exactly as I'd planned. "For your information, he's a roper." I said.

"Oh, well, that's impressive," Mitch said. "He's a goat roper."

I was there on a mission, so I ignored the sarcasm. "You know, I think it's about time you guys met him.

Y'all should let me bring him to one of your poker games. That would be really nice."

Uncle Ted raised his brows. "He likes poker, huh?"

I wasn't sure, but since this was my idea, I nodded.

They looked at one another. Mitch was the first to speak up. "Fair enough. I'll tell you what, he's welcome to join us for our next game. It's going to be at over at Buster's ranch, though. You remember Buster, Uncle Ted's buddy?" Mitch winked at Uncle Ted, who broke out in a shady grin.

I smiled. "Yes, I remember Buster. Great, we'll be there."

Gunner wouldn't look me in the eye. He rubbed his forehead and studied his cards.

Feeling pretty full of myself, I joined Grandma in the living room, but I overheard their faint conversation.

"Mitch, are you serious with this?" Gunner asked.

"She said he's a cowboy, and he likes poker." Mitch said.

"Alright, I'll set it up." Uncle Ted replied.

A week later, Lee and I arrived at Buster Conrad's ranch. I pointed toward the arena, where Uncle Ted and Buster chatted, wearing western hats. Mitch and Gunner wore theirs, too. I found this unusual, since they only wore cowboy hats for certain occasions: funerals, country & western dancing, and rodeos. Never for poker games.

As I made the introductions to Lee, another vehicle arrived. Lucas stepped from his pickup and walked our way.

He sported a cowboy hat, as he usually did, but this one was old and stained. I rushed to give him a hug.

"Lucas, come meet my boyfriend."

Lucas only half smiled, and offered Lee a firm handshake.

"I see you're wearing your lucky hat," Gunner asked Lucas. "Think you'll need it?"

Buster spoke up. "If everyone's ready to start, let's get this show on the road." He pointed to the middle of the arena, where a card table and four chairs were sitting. I got a sick feeling in my gut. I studied the faces of my cousins and Uncle Ted. Then I noticed Lee's alarmed expression. He stammered, "Umm, this wouldn't happen to be cowboy poker, would it?"

Buster laughed. "What did you think it was?" He whistled loudly to a cowboy he called "Lucky," who sprang into action. Lucky herded a bull into a fenced alley leading to the gate. The bull was big and mean-looking, with white horns and a deep black body.

The bull ran the length of the alley, then stopped just short of the chute. He dipped his head to peer between the fence rails, as if to size everyone up. Lucky whacked the metal fence to rush the bull along.

I remembered cowboy poker from rodeos I'd attended, usually with the Johnny Cash song "Ring of Fire" blaring through the sound system. Lee and I looked at one another nervously. I didn't let on that I was angry, but truth be known, I was ready to kill my cousins. What a dirty trick!

"You know the rules, right?' Mitch asked.

"Well, kinda'. I've never messed with bulls..." Lee said.

Mitch glanced at me. "I thought you said he's a cowboy?"

If my looks could kill, Mitch would be cold and in the ground.

"It's easy," Gunner slapped Lee on the back. "Last one to leave the table wins."

Mitch faked his concern. "Of course, if you're afraid of getting hurt, you can sit on the fence and watch."

Lee hesitated, looked at me and said, "Nah, its fine. I'll be all right."

I gave Uncle Ted a mean glance on my way to the fence. I climbed to the top rail and straddled it. He and Buster stood on the ground below me.

"What's the bull's name?" I asked.

Buster winked at me. "That's Lucifer."

"Just great." I whispered to myself.

Gunner, Lucas, Mitch, and Lee walked across the arena and seated themselves at the table. I wasn't sure whether to watch or shield my eyes. Lucky stood outside the gate and gave a thumbs up to the players. Mitch nodded. "We're ready."

Lucky heaved on the gate, taking care to stay behind it. The bull loped from the chute, kicked his back legs high and whipped them mid-air. Before Lucky could climb to safety, the bull's back legs crashed against the gate, which struck him in the chest. The blow seemed to knock the wind out of him, but he soon scrambled to the top of the fence.

Lucifer spotted Uncle Ted and Buster, lowered his head, and pawed at the dirt. I held my breath as Ted and Buster climbed the fence rails as fast as their old joints allowed, and were out of reach a mere second before he arrived.

The bull stopped, whipped its tail like a devil, and whirled around. From my place on the high fence, I could see the horror in Lee's face. I felt powerless to help him, and vowed silently to kill my cousins…If Lucifer didn't take them out first.

When Lucifer noticed the card table, he trotted forward, curious. He halted, lowered his head and snorted. I watched him paw the dirt three times. The poker players scooted to the edge of their seats.

Lucifer charged toward the table with a fury. Within a second, Lee came out of his chair and ran for the opposite fence. He didn't dare look back, which was a good thing. Just as Lee jumped for the fence rail, the bull clipped his right butt cheek, and tore off a back pocket. Lee almost fell, but managed to hang on for dear life.

I noticed a smirk on Mitch's face, which suddenly turned to fear as the bull set its sights on the table again. Lucifer circled them with his ears back, then dipped his horns and charged. Seconds later, the table was sky bound. I shrieked and turned my head away.

Gunner was knocked from his chair, and thrown flat on the dirt. Like a flash, he jumped to his feet and ran like a rabbit. The bull took after him, but appeared to change its mind. It spun around and caught sight of Mitch and Lucas, both still in their chairs.

Lucas, cool as a cucumber, flipped a card over and over in his fingers. He looked my way, then tucked the card under his hat band, and waited.

Lucifer charged, and butted Mitch's chair from behind. Mitch flew into the air and landed on his belly. The bull pushed its nose into Mitch's side, and scooted him across the ground a few inches. Mitch remained motionless. I was fearful that the bull had hurt him, despite my hard feelings.

Lucas leapt from his chair and acted as a rodeo clown by waving his arms. He lured the bull away from Mitch, and then it chased him to the gate. Lucas flipped the latch, then jumped from the beast's path. The bull stalled, looked back at Mitch—as he attempted to stand up—then trotted back into the chute. Lucas slammed the gate behind him.

Since the card players were on their feet, and appeared unhurt, I felt the sudden need to be a smartass. I crossed my arms over my chest and yelled out, "Wow, wasn't that fun?"

Buster walked over to Lucas, lifted one of his arms, and declared him the winner of the game. Later, I could barely control my amusement as Mitch limped all the way to his truck. Lee was anxious to leave as well. His pride a little hurt, no doubt, he asked if I could find another ride home.

He didn't bother to kiss me goodbye. I asked Lucas for a ride.

We laughed about the night's events on the way. When we stopped in my parent's driveway, he turned a little melancholy. I could tell something was on his mind.

"Everything okay?" I asked.

He pulled on the door handle. "Yeah. I'll walk with you."

I turned to face him when we reached the gate. He gazed into my eyes. The moon hung low in the sky behind him. "Are you in love with that guy?"

I sighed. "I'm not sure. How do you know when you're in love?"

He leaned on the gate. "Hard to say, probably feels different from person to person. To me, it's like you've been living in winter for a really long time, and then one day, spring comes. The whole world just sorta' brightens up. It feels so warm, and you want it to last forever. The thought of winter coming back is unbearable."

I stared at him in wonder. "Wow. That's incredible. It sounds like you're in love."

He looked down at his boots and smiled. "Sorry, didn't mean to sound all mushy."

"No, it was beautiful," I touched his arm. "I take my relationship with Lee seriously, but I can't say that I'm in love. Maybe in time?"

Lucas pulled the card from his hatband and handed it to me. The queen of hearts.

"Here's a souvenir."

He returned to his truck and left me alone with the moon.

On Christmas Eve, Steven closed the pharmacy early. It was just the two of us that day, and he rushed to lock the doors as soon as the clock hit twelve. Then he motioned me to the break area. When I walked in the room, he held up a bottle and two glasses. "Have you ever tried champagne?"

I nodded. "Yes, at Mitch and Valerie's wedding. I took a few sips when my mom wasn't looking."

"Come, let's make a toast."

He poured, and we raised our glasses together.

"To us," he said, "and many Christmases to come."

I sipped my champagne. Its bubbles stung my tongue until the bitterness gave way to sweet. Steven refilled our glasses, generously this time, all the way to the top. After the second glass, I felt warm all over. I'd always looked forward to glamourous moments like this.

Steven gestured to a chair. "Sit for a while."

He switched off the overheads, which left only the Christmas lights to illuminate the room.

"I have something for you." He reached into a pocket and pulled out a small velvet box.

I sort of panicked. "Oh gosh, I didn't get—"

He placed a finger on my lips. "It's fine, I don't need anything."

He dropped the box into my palm. Sweat beaded up across my nose. I opened the lid and gasped. "Diamond earrings? Oh my God, seriously?" I couldn't take my eyes off of them, even long enough to notice him slide into the chair beside mine.

He leaned close. "You amaze me, Sara. That's why I wanted to give you something special."

A giant pang of guilt overcame me. I closed the box and scooted my chair backward.

"You're the best, Steven. And, I appreciate you, but I can't accept your gift."

He pushed the strands of hair from my shoulder. His voice was soft and sexy as he begged. "Please, I want you to have them. They'll look beautiful on you. I guess you might have noticed how attracted I am to you…With your pretty smile and those gorgeous brown eyes. God, I think about you all the time."

I stood. "Thanks, for the nice compliments, Steven. I really hate to run out on our celebration, but I promised to help Mom with our holiday baking."

I hurried to the back to retrieve my coat, and swung it over my shoulders. Steven's hands were suddenly around my waist. I shrieked in alarm.

He held up a finger to shush me. "Sorry. I didn't mean to startle you. I just wanted to hug you goodbye."

A bad feeling came over me, as I struggled for something casual to say. "I'm sure your family is ready to have you home." I gave him the briefest hug of my entire life and pulled away from his arms.

He walked me to the door and unlocked it. "I wish you could stay longer, but I understand. I know you're close to your family. Please don't mention the earrings, okay? Let's keep it between us?"

I faked a smile. "Merry Christmas."

I drove straight home and tried not to think about my encounter with Steven. After Mom and I finished our baking, I went to my bedroom to wait for Lee's nightly call. 9 pm rolled around, with no call. I lifted the receiver to check for a dial tone, but the phone was working fine. Who said the guy had to do all the calling anyway? It was the 1970's, for crying out loud. Impatient, I dialed his number.

Lee's mother answered the phone and gave me a royal chewing out.

"No, Lee is not here. He went out. I don't know why you girls are so disrespectful. Please, don't ring my house again after 9 p.m."

Why had she said, "*You girls*?" I was stunned. But before I could explain myself, she hung up on me. After my uncomfortable experience at the pharmacy, I really needed to hear Lee's voice. Instead, I called Gillie for a little positive reinforcement.

"Lee's momma doesn't sound very nice," she said. "By the way, I talked to Billy Jack earlier. He keeps calling and bugging me to go out with him. I probably shouldn't mention this, but Billy Jack seems to think that Lee is hanging out with another girl."

I was puzzled. "Who is she?"

"I don't know her name, but he said she's older."

"Hanging out or dating her?" I asked, as tears welled up in my eyes.

Gillie was confused. "Huh?"

I had a gut feeling there was more to her story. "What have you left out, Gillie?"

She was briefly silent.

"Are you psychic or something?" she asked. "Alright, but please don't take this the wrong way. Billy Jack told me that Lee prefers older, more experienced girls, and not so much the goody-two-shoes type."

It felt like someone slapped me in the face. Tears spilled down my cheeks.

"Sara, don't cry…I don't think Billy Jack meant that towards you."

My temper flared. "What an asshole!"

Gillie tried to soften the blow. "Who cares what those guys think anyway? I wouldn't consider Lee a huge loss."

"I thought I meant something to him," I cried.

Gillie did her best to comfort me. "Oh my God. I'm on your side, okay?"

I wiped away my tears. "Well, who needs a little boy when I can have a grown man?"

Gillie's tone changed. "Would this grown man happen to be Steven?"

I was hurt and angry, so I told Gillie about the champagne and diamonds. I also shared details about Steven's unhappy marriage, and I boasted about his attraction to me. I could almost hear the wheels turning inside her head. She proceeded carefully. "Look, let's not jump the gun.

We don't know that has Lee cheated on you. He could be totally innocent and roping calves with his friends right now. Starting up an affair with a married man is not the cure for your pain. Promise you won't make any hasty decisions."

I checked my makeup in the mirror. "Well, I'm not sitting at home. Get dressed up cause I'm coming to get you. We're going to The Foxhole tonight."

I grabbed the shortest dress I owned, a red one with polka dots. I held it close and studied my reflection in the mirror. This might remedy my "goody-two-shoes" reputation, I thought. I slipped it over my head and popped open the first three buttons. Still, something was amiss. I pulled a black leather jacket off a hanger, and chose a pair of boots. Now for the final touch, the new diamond studs. With my outfit complete, I smiled at myself in the mirror. "Yeah."

I skirted past my parents, who were so fascinated with a TV show, they didn't notice me at all.

"Going to Gillie's." I announced as I bounced out the door.

Gillie was waiting at her gate when I arrived. She jumped in and let out a gasp.

"Damn girl, your titties are practically in my face!"

Gillie did her best to cheer me up, and we laughed the whole four-mile drive.

"I can't wait to see my sister's face when we walk in the bar. And your cousins, too. Their jaws will probably hit the floor. Do you think they'll make us leave?"

I shook my head. "No…Gunner has invited me before. It'll be fine."

"Since you and I aren't exactly barflies," Gillie said, "we'll be the talk of the town tomorrow. You just watch." She laughed and belted out a Tammy Wynette song about a good girl going bad.

I laughed so hard I could barely drive. "Gillie, please stop before I pee on myself."

We pulled into the crowded parking lot. "The Foxhole" sign flashed in neon green. Music blared, and according to the noise that spilled outside, the place was definitely rocking. I grabbed Gillian's hand and took a deep breath. "Momma's gonna' kill me when she finds out."

We ran together, then paused at the bar's double doors.

"Are you ready for this, Gillie?"

She gave me her naughtiest grin, "Let's knock 'em dead."

We turned heads as we strutted past the bar. There was only one vacant table to choose from, so we sat down and removed our jackets. Pete, the bartender, did a double-take and walked over. "Well hello ladies. What can I get for you tonight?"

"Hi Pete." I answered, "Two long necks, please?"

He gave me a suspicious nod. "Does Gunner know you're here?"

I cut my eyes at him. "Gunner's not my daddy, now is he?"

Word must have spread pretty quickly, because Paulette appeared out of nowhere.

"What the hell are y'all doing here?" she asked.

Gillie attempted an explanation. "Well, it's the holiday season."

Paulette glared at my cleavage, then pulled out a chair to join us. "Sara, does Gunner know you're here?"

I shook my head in disbelief. "I'm going to the lady's room. Be right back."

Once in the bathroom, I stood in front of the mirror and dug into my purse for the Vixen red lipstick that Steven liked so much. I applied it generously, spritzed myself with cologne, then flew out the bathroom door—right into Lucas's chest. He fumbled for an apology, then realized it was me. His eyes grew large when he looked down to see our chests pressed together. "Sara?"

Eager for a reaction to my newfound image, I attempted a seductive smile. "Hi handsome! Like my dress?" I intentionally brushed against him, then walked away. He stood there for a moment, possibly in shock.

When I returned to the table, I found Gillie sitting alone. She passed me a beer. "Paulette went outside to smoke."

"Guess who I ran into? Lucas." I laughed.

"Oh, your future husband?"

I slapped the table with my palm. "No, girl! It's not like that."

She grinned big. "Oh, Sara…He's so in love with you. I can tell. You really should take him more seriously."

I took a large swig of beer. "Since you've chosen my husband, let me look around and pick one for you."

She peered over her shoulder and scanned the bar. "I don't think he's here yet. Paulette is taking forever. What's she doing out there? "

"Well, there's a full moon, so she's probably getting laid." I pretended to howl like a wolf.

"Just Got Paid" by ZZ Top bellowed from the sound system. The crowd was getting rowdy. Just as I took a swig from my beer, someone tapped on the shoulder. I spun around to find Mitch hovering over me. "I need you for a minute."

He glanced at Gillie. "She'll be right back."

I grabbed my beer, but Mitch snatched it away and placed it back on the table. Gillie's eyes were as large as saucers. I filed behind him towards Gunner's office, which was down the hall, and just past the bathrooms. Mitch closed the door behind us. Lucas leaned against a file cabinet in the corner. Gunner was seated at a large desk. He pointed to a chair. "Hey Sara, have a seat."

Though I had only consumed half of my beer, the buzz was setting in. A little saucy, I seized the opportunity to poke some fun. "Good Lord, Gunner, you look like the Godfather. And I'll stand, thank you. Gillie's waiting for me."

Gunner raised his brows. "Do your folks know you're here?"

I folded my arms and rolled eyes. "I'm not a child anymore. What's this about?"

I could tell from Mitch's expression that he wanted to speak, but Gunner kept the floor. "Something has been called to my attention,"

"Can we hurry this along? I came here to have some fun." I said.

Gunner leaned forward. "What's with the attitude? You're not being judged."

Before I knew it could leap from my mouth, it had already leapt. "Oh, really now? For your information, I don't need your permission to drink a beer or show my cleavage."

Lucas looked away, but I knew he was concealing a laugh.

Gunner sighed. "You think this is about your boobs?"

I shrugged. "What the hell else could it be about? I'm 18 now, which means I can legally be here."

Mitch placed both hands on the back of his head and pressed his lips together. It seemed he was about to lose his cool, but he spoke in a low and controlled tone. "We want to know, what's the deal with your boss?"

I looked at each of them. What could they possibly know? My best defense was to play dumb. "Steven? What do you mean?"

The veins became visible in Mitch's neck, which usually signaled an impending meltdown. His voiced became stern. "I mean, what's going on between you two?"

I shot back. "I don't know, Mitch. What's going on with you and your wife?"

His lips parted, but he was rendered speechless. You would've thought I'd pulled a gun on him.

Gunner made another attempt. "Sara, I'm just gonna' cut right to it. Has the guy been inappropriate?"

The nerve of them! Regret it or not, I was about to teach them a lesson for meddling. "It isn't considered inappropriate when you're both willing, right."

Mitch raised his voice, full meltdown now in progress. "We know he bought the diamonds, Sara! Do I have to remind you that he's a married man?"

I pointed at his chest. "Maybe it's you who needs a reminder? You're the one who stays out all night while Valerie waits up for you."

He slammed his hand down on Gunner's desk. "I don't believe this shit."

Gunner stood. "Look, we're just trying to watch out for you, that's all."

I'd suffered enough for one day. My fangs came out. "Watching out for me? I call it interfering." Then I directed my anger straight at Mitch. "What's that old saying about glass houses?"

He raised a finger that I knew was about to be in my face. But before he got to me, I raced out the door and back to Gillie. "Let's find another bar," I said, "My cousins are being assholes."

About that time, Pete dimmed the lights and flipped on the disco ball. The song "Lowdown" by Boz Scaggs started on the sound system. Mitch came huffing down the hallway and spotted me. I turned my back to him, and reached for my jacket and purse. His hand clutched my arm. "You can leave after we've settled this," he said.

He pulled me towards the dance floor. I wondered whether he was high or had lost his damned mind. "Are you crazy?"

He gave me a smirk. "Just a little bit."

He held out his hand, as if an offer to dance. I grimaced and tried to leave him on the spot, but after only one step, his arms were around my waist. He lifted me and carried me to the middle of the dance floor. I became frantic and looked around for help. Lucas took notice, and had started my way, but Gunner intercepted him. "Let them be."

Mitch pulled me close. "Just give me a minute," he said. "Don't leave yet."

"You're such a jackass!" I said, with tears in my eyes.

He lifted my hand up and spun me out, then reeled me back in. On the return, I lost my balance and almost fell.

He shook his head and scolded, "Come on now. I taught you better than that."

I was determined to give him hell. "I really hate your guts right now," I said through gritted teeth.

"You came here for some fun. Here we go!" He led me so fast I could barely keep up. His dance techniques had certainly improved, but he still couldn't hold a candle to Lucas. Mitch whirled me from one end of the floor to the other, and so quickly that my head spun.

Then he flashed a devilish smile. "You know you can't stay mad at me."

Deep inside I knew it was true. By mid-song, I had finally loosened up. It felt so good to be lost in the music. I glimpsed at my table, where Lucas stood, nursing a beer and dancing in place. Gillie raised her third longneck and nodded. Paulette, on the other hand, looked as if she'd eaten an unripe persimmon. That's when it came together in my mind. Gillie must have told Paulette about the diamonds, and Paulette ratted me out to Mitch and Gunner.

As the song died down, Mitch steered me into a corner and leaned close to my ear. My heart raced as I wondered what was next. I could feel the moistness of his breath. His voice was smooth and intoxicating. "Button up your dress."

A little charmed, I did as I was told.

"Listen," he said. "I can't help what people say about me. Some of it's true, some isn't. But I care what you think, and you have to believe this; I don't cheat on my wife."

He whirled me out and reeled me in.

"Okay, I believe you."

We stood still and he looked into my eyes. "I'm glad we have that out of the way. Now, I want you to keep this in the back of your mind; if I hear your boss-man has touched you again, I'm gonna' kill him."

I blinked at the seriousness of his threat, and in a flash, he released me and was gone. The situation was far more serious than I had imagined. I swallowed hard and tried to gather my wits, then headed toward the table where Gillie waited.

Lucas called out as I rushed off the dancefloor. "You okay, Sara?"

I turned and nodded, still dazed by Mitch's words. Lucas came closer. "Would you like to dance with me?"

I rudely brushed him off. "No thanks. I believe I've had enough fun for one night. You can tell your buddies I'm going home now."

After I climbed into bed that night, my arrogant behavior returned to haunt me. Never had I spoken to my cousins or Lucas with such disrespect. And the worst part is, I'd led them to believe I had slept with Steven. My stomach hurt. I pulled my knees to my chest and hugged them tightly.

Then my thoughts drifted to Lee, and my heart felt heavy. Now I understood the reason behind sad love songs. He was probably with someone else right now. Someone prettier, maybe, and more experienced.

I pulled my headphones from the bedside table, placed them over my ears, and turned the music way up. Maybe it would help to ease my sadness. That's when it hit me…Tomorrow's Christmas! I'd have to face Gunner, Mitch, and Lucas at dinner. Horrified, I pulled a pillow over my head. "Oh, shit!"

Contrary to my expectations, Christmas day went smoothly, and my cousins didn't mention a word about the night before. As Grandma said Grace, I sensed eyes upon me. I looked up to confirm what I already knew, it was Mitch. Was he disappointed in me? Valerie was beside him, her head bowed and eyes closed. For some reason, she didn't seem her usual self. I lowered my eyes and looked at my lap for the remainder of the prayer.

After the meal, everyone scattered. I went to Grandma's phone and dialed Gillie, who was still wound tight from our night at The Foxhole. It's all she could talk about, until I eventually interrupted her. "You told your sister, didn't you? Please don't tell her my business anymore, Gillie. She ratted me out to my cousins, I'm sure of it. What a bitch!"

I felt someone behind me. Gunner placed a finger on the phone hook, then pushed it down to cut us off. "That's enough, Sara. Just let it go."

Not exactly in the best place for an argument, I attempted my best pout. "It was Paulette, wasn't it? She told you."

"Nice try. But, you're always welcome back at The Foxhole. No drama, please?" He broke into a grin. "Merry Christmas."

As Gunner was about to walk out the door, Lucas arrived. As with all holidays, he celebrated with his own family early, then came to be with us, his second family. He shook hands with Gunner and they exchanged greetings. Lucas nodded at me, but without his usual smile. The phone rang; it was Gillie, who accused me of hanging up on her.

"No, I didn't!" I promised. "We'll have to talk about this later." Then I hung up on her, purposely this time.

Guilt ate at me as I approached Lucas. "Can I see you on the porch?"

He didn't answer, but followed me to the swing, where we sat together.

"Dang, it's cold, isn't it?" I asked. "How's your Christmas? Was Santa good to you?" Despite my cheery efforts, I was unsuccessful at getting a smile from him.

He didn't make eye contact. "It's been good, mostly."

Key word, mostly. He made small talk. "I'm going back to Wyoming tomorrow. It'll be a hard drive with all the snow up there."

I wasn't about to let him leave without my apology. I had an idea. "I need to get out of here. Maybe I'll take a drive up in the hills. Wanna' come?"

His eyes met mine. I didn't give him much of a chance to think about it. "Go say hi to everyone and then meet me at the Jeep."

He seemed a little unsure, but I channeled the charm that Mitch used on me the night before. I leaned close and whispered in his ear. "Please come with me, Lucas."

I waited in my Jeep until Lucas reappeared on the porch. As he headed my way, I found myself in admiration of him. His long hair was loose, rather than in a pony tail or under a hat. He wore a western shirt underneath his khaki jacket, and a pair of starched jeans. After he slid into the passenger seat, he buckled up and gave me a nod. It was cold, but we rolled down the windows for the drive. The air smelled of cedar and smoke that day. "I have a few beers in my cooler," I said. "Let's find a place to go kick around."

He raised his brows. "You're carrying around beer? When did you become a party girl?"

"My boyfriend, I mean ex, left them in here. I'm sure they're still cold."

He was eager to hear more. "Oh? What's-his-name, Lee? You broke up? When did this happen?"

I explained in detail as we drove along. It was important that he knew the events leading to my behavior at the bar.

"So, does this mean it's over between you?" he asked.

I sighed. "Well, we didn't actually have a fight. He hasn't called, though."

"Could mean he's just busy, holidays and all. Turn right just over the hill," Lucas pointed ahead. "There's a bridge a little way down. Uncle Ted used to take us fishing there."

I crossed the bridge and pulled off to the side. He grabbed the cooler and I followed him to a line of large boulders that overlooked the river. He climbed onto one of them and reached to help me up. Wild birds chirped and sang in the trees around us. Lucas and I sat to face one another, then he grabbed two beers from the cooler. We popped them open, and he waited for me to speak.

"Actually, I heard from a good source that Lee is see-ing someone else. I'm sure it's over between us. Gut feel-ing, I guess."

"Is that why you brought me here? You needed some-one to talk to?" he asked.

"No, well…Not entirely."

Lucas seemed to read my mind. "Sometimes it's good to get things off your chest, right?"

I placed a hand on my chest and smoothed out my snug red sweater. "Hmm, I don't know, I kinda' like my chest just the way it is."

He chuckled. "Yeah, I like it, too."

I took a swig from my beer and contemplated my apol-ogy. It was best to jump in headfirst. "I'm very sorry, Lu-cas."

He wrinkled his brow, "You're sorry? For what?"

Now I was the confused one. "I acted like a brat last night. Believe me, I regret it. The last thing I want is for you to think badly of me."

"Actually, I can't blame you for being upset."

This was going much easier than I'd expected. "I really don't know why Paulette caused all of the trouble between us. That girl has some nerve."

He shifted a little. "Paulette?"

"Come on, admit it. I've got it all figured out. She told my cousins about the diamonds."

The cat came out of the bag. "Well, that's not exactly how it went," Lucas admitted. "She was planning to tell them, but she came to me first. She claimed to be concerned for you."

"Concerned?" I laughed. "Come on."

"Mitch was under the influence, so to speak. I knew he'd be pissed, but I had no idea he'd behave like he did. Believe me, I feel terrible about it."

"You feel terrible? Why?"

Lucas took a deep breath. "Because it was me. I told Mitch, then he went to Gunner."

My heart sank. Lucas betrayed me, of all people. I got a sick feeling in my gut. The woods were suddenly silent around us.

Lucas nudged my leg with his boot. "Sara?"

I refused to look at him.

"I know you're disappointed," he said, "but you're missing the point."

I stood up and came back to life. "Well then why don't you clue me in? Tell me the reason you stabbed me in the back?"

He threw his beer and jumped to his feet. "You don't see it, girl?"

We'd never faced off in our lives, but I held my own. "What I see is a bunch of people up in my damned business."

But Lucas shot right back. "Why would a married man give you diamond earrings? Because you're nice to him? Because you're a good employee? Are you that naïve? He's taking advantage of you, Sara."

I yelled, "You jumped the gun, Lucas!"

He shook his head. "I was right there, and you didn't deny it."

I pointed my finger. "I haven't slept with Steven, although you guys have practically painted a red "A" on my chest."

He shook his head. "Why didn't you reveal this last night?"

I shrugged my shoulders. "I don't know, it's like one minute I'm a goody-two-shoes, the next I'm a whore. I'm treated like a kid, but expected to act like an adult. What does everyone want from me?"

Lucas cursed under his breath. "Right now, I want to take you over my knee."

I jumped down and walked to the water's edge. I was so angry, I considered leaving him to walk all the way home. I didn't hear his approach, but I could feel him near…Close enough to touch.

"All right," he said, "I take full responsibility for what happened last night. I should have kept my big mouth shut. But Sara, you have to know how fortunate you are. Mitch and Gunner truly want what's best for you. They love you."

His footsteps trailed away. "And so do I."

I rolled my eyes. There it was. He just had to go and say it. What was I going to do with his revelation? I stalled for a minute, and stooped to touch the chilly water. I looked over my shoulder. Lucas was leaning on the hood of my Jeep with his back to me.

Something strange came over me, and I feared that I could lose him. It was really no secret that he cared for me. I had known way before anyone else. Yet all this time, I'd refused to take his feelings to heart. Confusion gripped me, but I had to make things right. I stood and walked to him, wrapped my arms around his waist and pressed myself into his back. I could hear his heartbeat, and in that moment, I completely forgave him. "You've always been the peacekeeper," I said, "and I know you meant well."

He broke my grip and turned to face me. "You don't have to say anything."

"My cousins still see me as a child, but I'm all grown up now," I said.

Lucas nodded. "I'm quite aware of that."

"Can I ask you a favor? If you hear anymore rumors, will you come to me first?"

"Yes, and I'm sorry this came between us," he said.

I took his hands in mine. "Nothing will come between us, Lucas. Not if I have anything to do with it."

That night, Gillie came to my house for a sleepover. We lay sprawled in front of the Christmas tree with fashion magazines and a big box of chocolates. I lit a pine-scented candle on the coffee table.

"Where are your parents tonight?" Gillie asked.

"Visiting Aunt Katie and Uncle Stan. They're probably playing cards or a board game."

Gillie pouted. "Are you still mad at me and Paulette? I'm sorry if we caused you trouble. I didn't intend for that to happen, and I don't believe she did either. She really likes you."

She rolled onto her back and stared up at the blinking lights.

I walked to the living room window and gazed outside. The wind howled, as a winter front moved in.

"I'm not mad at you, Gillie, but I need to be able to trust you. I realize you were worried about me, but I hope you'll keep details about my life to yourself. I don't enjoy conflicts with my cousins and Lucas."

She sat up quickly. "Lucas? The two of you had a fight? When?"

I turned from the window. "Earlier today. We're okay now, though. He admitted everything, that Paulette told him what she'd heard about the diamonds, and that she was going to tell my cousins. But Lucas took it into his own hands."

Gillie's eyes widened. "Did you yell at him?"

"Yeah. And believe it or not, he yelled back," I said.

Her expression turned to shock. "*Nooo!*"

I nodded. "Seriously. I must have really pushed his buttons. And then, get this, he said that he loves me."

Gillie's jaw dropped. She was momentarily speechless.

I paced back and forth. "I should be flattered, and it's not like I don't admire him. He's probably one of the best guys I've ever met. I value our friendship, but I'm not sure I want it to change. Even if I were to give him a chance, he'd probably move back here right away and want to get married and have babies." I faced her. "I want more than that. Do you know what I mean?"

"I think you worry too much."

I attempted to explain. "A career, Gillie. That's what I want. And I want to see more of the world before I settle down."

Gillie shook her head. "Well, Lucas lives in Wyoming. You could always move up there. And what makes you think you can't have it all? Oh Sara, why do you stress about these things? I think if you gave Lucas a chance, he might just surprise you."

I shrugged and crinkled my nose. "It sounds so perfect, it's almost boring. Does that even make sense? Aren't relationships supposed to be like a roller coaster ride?"

She frowned. "I certainly hope not. Just be honest with him. If you're not interested, he'll accept it and go on with his life. I'm sure he's a great catch for someone else."

I bit my lip at the thought. It actually stung a little.

A week later, 1976 drifted in, quiet and uneventful. The roads were still icy and treacherous from the winter storm just days before. Gillie and I chatted on the phone while watching Dick Clark's New Year's Rockin' Eve on tv.

"It's unusual for my parents to be home tonight. They normally have plans with Uncle Stan and Aunt Katie on New Year's Eve. I wonder if things are rocking at The Foxhole?" I said.

Gillie sighed. "Too bad we're not there to see for ourselves."

"I know. I'm so bored I could scream. It'll be nice to have the day off tomorrow. Steven has been playing on my nerves."

"How's that?" Gillie asked.

"The other day, he confronted me at work, and asked why I hadn't mentioned Lee lately. I told him that our relationship had fizzled out. He wanted details, but honestly, I didn't feel like going into it with him."

"Did he drop the subject?"

"I believe he got the point, but he offered his shoulder to cry on. I thanked him and told him I'm just fine."

"Good for you," Gillie said.

"I rarely even think about Lee anymore," I told her. "I'm not interested in Steven, either. Truth be known, he makes it hard for me to enjoy my job."

"Is he harassing you, Sara?"

"I wouldn't call it that. Not yet anyway. Some days I dread going to work, though."

Gillie warned me. "Don't put up with it, girl. Set some boundaries with him."

I agreed. "I might have to."

"Did Lucas go back to Wyoming?" she asked.

"Yes, and speaking of Lucas, he called today to wish me a happy new year. Sweet, huh?"

Gillie giggled. "Yeah, very sweet."

A few months later, spring arrived like a pastel parade. Jonquils and hyacinths popped from the ground, dogwood trees budded, and a thousand shades of green blanketed the fields. We had our first storm, which blew away a neighbor's chicken house. Thankfully, it was unoccupied at the time.

I'd been taught early in life to pay attention to the weather report. When storms were predicted, I usually spent the night with Grandma Janie, as she needed support climbing up and down the cellar steps. Mom and Aunt Katie feared that she'd fall, and tried to convince her to move in with either of them. She told them no, and said she wanted to remain in her own home as long as possible.

One particular Friday night, I packed a tote bag and drove to the farm. Grandma was watching the sky when I arrived, and pointed to the distant lightning. "Most of the bad ones come from that direction," she said.

We went inside to prepare for a long night. She instructed me to grab pillows and a blanket, while she placed a Mason jar full of water next to her lantern. Our rain jackets were close by. All set, we settled on the sofa to watch TV with popcorn and Dr. Peppers. Beeping weather alerts continuously crossed the top of the television screen.

Within half an hour, a strong wind howled a warning of its own. "It's time," Grandma said.

She turned off the tv and handed me my raincoat. We pulled up our hoods and hurried outside. Thunder roared as we crossed the yard. We made our way to the cellar, which sat adjacent to the garden area.

I lifted the heavy wooden door and helped Grandma Janie inside. As I attempted to close the door, a sheet of rain blew into my face. I grabbed the handle with both hands and pulled down firmly.

Grandma Janie patted the bench beside her. "Come here, Sara."

We sat close together, hoping the storm would quickly pass us. But the wind had other plans. We could hear it roaring in the treetops. Suddenly, there was a loud thump. And then another.

I tightened my grip on Grandma's hand. "What was that sound? Do you think a limb fell?"

She shook her head. "No, I don't believe so." She pointed up, "It sounded like the door."

There was another thump, accompanied by a yell.

My heart raced. "Someone's out there."

"Go child, unlatch the door. Quickly!"

I rushed up the steps, unlocked the door and pushed it up with my shoulder. A dark figure stood alone, unwavering in the gale-forced wind. "Mitch?" I called out.

He jumped in and pulled the door shut.

"Got caught in the storm, huh?" Grandma said. "Need a blanket?"

He shook his head. "No, I'm fine."

I remained quiet, but studied his expression; agitated and a little lost. He came closer. "Slumber party? How long have y'all been down in this hole?"

Grandma looked at her watch. "About twenty minutes. Why?"

"Hell, it's not even bad out there," he said. "You don't need to run down here every time lightning strikes. The steps are really steep."

I wondered what was up with him. What a jerk.

Grandma must've shared my thought. She waggled a finger at him. "Young man, I'll have you know that I'm able get around well enough. I know what storms can do. There's a reason I'm this old."

He laughed. "I don't doubt you, Grandma. But not all storms require a trip to the cellar." His gaze fell on me, then back to her. "Have you ever watched one play out? It can be quite beautiful."

Grandma listened without batting an eye.

Mitch shook the rain from his dark hair, then walked to a corner. He eased into a chair, and gripped its arms with both hands. He leaned back and stretched his legs. I watched the rise and fall of his chest. One side of his face was shadowed. Reflections of the lantern's flame danced in his eyes. He reminded me of a vampire; beautiful, yet dangerous. My muscles tightened, and a shiver came from nowhere.

I broke my own silence. "Where's Valerie? Hopefully not being blown away?"

Mitch gazed at the concrete floor. "I'm not sure. I haven't seen her since last week."

I wanted to curse him, but Grandma stepped in. "I'm sorry, honey. I hate to hear that."

Mitch stood. "Listen." He placed a finger on his lips.

Grandma and I exchanged glances.

"The storm's died down," Mitch said. "Let's go. I'm getting claustrophobic."

Since when, I wondered? Of all the trips we'd made to the cellar, he never complained of claustrophobia.

Outside, I looked for his truck, but didn't see it. Once in the house, Grandma kissed us goodnight and went to bed. Mitch motioned me to the porch.

"Did you walk here?" I asked.

"No," He pointed to the back of the house. "I parked behind the barn. Why do you ask these things?"

I was perplexed. "Hiding from someone?"

His answer seemed evasive. "The wolf is always at the door, Sara. But I'm getting used to it."

Patience wasn't my virtue, especially tonight. It was time to acknowledge his behavior. "What the hell is wrong?" I asked. "You've been so different lately."

He gave me that look, it made me feel vulnerable.

"If you must know, I had a round with Chester earlier."

I was lost. "Chester?"

"Lance's right-hand man," he explained. "We have different ideas, you could say."

I dug for more information. "Different ideas about the bar?"

Mitch changed the subject. "So, why weren't you out having fun instead of being holed up underground with Grandma?"

"I try to watch out for her. And besides," I reminded him, "having fun seems to land me in trouble."

He reached for my chin. "Oh, poor baby."

I gently pulled away.

He chuckled. "Have I made you uncomfortable?"

"To say the least," I told him.

"I remember when you actually looked up to me. I was your protector. Things have obviously changed. Now you see me as a fool."

I couldn't hold back. "Maybe it's you that needs a protector?" I didn't intend for my words to be abrasive. Well, maybe I did. But I'll never forget the look on his face.

The rain stopped, but distant thunder rumbled on. A fierce wind indicated that we weren't out of the woods yet.

A wave of guilt washed over me. "Look, it really breaks my heart that Valerie left. Can't you fix this?"

He took a deep breath. "It's not my fault she has trust issues."

I frowned and looked the other way.

Mitch snapped, "Goddamnit! Please don't do that."

"Do what?" I demanded.

"That look of pity or disgust? Who knows?"

How dare he make me out to be the bad guy. "You see me as the enemy, when all I want is what's best for you. Do you think I take pleasure in your agony?"

He scolded me, "*Ssshhh*…Keep it down, you'll wake Grandma."

"Me? You're telling me to keep it down?"

I knew there was no reasoning with him. Our conversation had come to a dead end.

He leaned back and looked at the ceiling.

"You don't need to worry about me, Sara. I've made it through everything else, haven't I?"

I turned my back to him, frustrated. A minute or two must have passed before I spoke. "I'm going to bed. I'll grab a blanket if you'd like to stay?"

His reply was laced with sarcasm. "Aren't you a good little keeper. Grandma has trained you well. I might stay and watch the sky a while. You know how unpredictable storms are."

Despite everything, I couldn't go to bed mad at him. "I'm sorry. I didn't mean to…"

He held up a hand. "No, its fine. Really."

"Goodnight, Mitch. I love you."

When Grandma and I woke the following morning, he was gone. The blanket was still where I'd left it, neatly folded.

Uncle Ted's health continued to deteriorate. After much thought and with a heavy heart, he sold the Appaloosas to a neighbor. He believed it was best for the horses. Though I begged him to reconsider, he reasoned with me, "My neighbor has a couple of teenagers who'll ride them and keep them worked out. Besides, I can look out my window and watch them every day."

Grandma rarely made it to church anymore. Arthritis had developed in her hips and knees. She complained of joint pain often, and spent more time in the recliner. On good days, she still puttered around her yard and garden, careful not to overdo herself.

After Lucas returned to Wyoming, he stayed in touch by calling me every weekend. Our conversations were a cozy place to unwind. We confided our struggles and shared our dreams. While I longed to move away, he hoped to eventually move back home. He talked about opening a horse training outfit in Oklahoma, and to help reach this goal, he was working two jobs. He worked full-time in construction during the week, and on weekends, he trained cutting horses for a local rancher. He hadn't visited us in months. During one of our late-night conversations, I detected a loneliness in his voice. "Why don't you come visit?" I asked. "You've been gone for too long."

Lucas seemed flattered with my suggestion, and jumped to make the preparations. I had developed a new and strange obsession, though I refused to take it seriously. It was all about Lucas' voice, which had grown deep and smooth with maturity. My stance on being just friends hadn't changed, but I found myself thinking of him at the oddest of times. Not only that, but sometimes our chats left me aroused. I didn't let on, and kept it strictly to myself.

Per Gillie's sister Paulette, a rumor was flying around town about Mitch. Gillie shared the hearsay with me, that Mitch was using "crank." And despite his recent behavior, I refused to believe it. After all, Paulette wasn't the best of sources. I asked Gillie, "What is crank?"

"Paulette said it's a drug called methamphetamine that you snort. Similar to cocaine."

I shook my head, "No. My cousin drinks a little and smokes marijuana, but he would never do that."

Gillie shrugged. "I hope you're right, Sara."

The Foxhole's first anniversary was coming up, so Gunner asked me to help him prepare for the event. He planned an entire weekend of festivities: food and drink specials, live music, dance contests, and pool tournaments. He had just given his two weeks' notice at the mill. The Foxhole was off to a great start, and Gunner seemed genuinely happy.

Gunner joined a local gym and was working out often. His appearance began to change. The clean-cut soldier look was gone, swapped for a full beard and hair that reached his collar. His wardrobe was more current with the mid-70s scene; such as fitted shirts in eye-catching patterns, corduroy jeans, and sometimes a blazer. His new style reminded me of Barry Gibb.

Meanwhile, I tried to keep the peace. I did my best to ward Steven off. I learned to avoid being alone with him, and became less available when he needed someone to talk to. It didn't take long for him to put two and two together. One day, he approached me as I stocked the cosmetic shelves. He hovered for a few moments, then spoke. "Your Grandma is popular, isn't she? I hear our customers asking you about her often."

I smiled up at him. "Yes, she's everyone's grandma."

"Sounds like a great lady. I'd like to meet her," his voice was thick with desperation. "Maybe you and I could drive out to her farm soon?"

I tried to visualize how that might go over with my cousins. Like a ton of bricks.

I stammered, "Or, umm…I could bring her here for a milkshake someday?"

I stood, picked up an empty box, and carried it to the storage room at the back of the pharmacy. I put the box beside a trash can, then turned to find Steven inches away. "I've been waiting for the right moment," he said.

I froze.

He reached to touch my bottom lip. "I felt an attraction between us on the day we met."

I turned my face away. "I can't."

His eyes undressed me. "You're so cute and petite. You have a beautiful body, Sara." His lips glazed my cheek as I pulled back.

"This isn't right, Steven. I need to go now."

His voice followed behind me as I walked away. "Why are you denying yourself? Despite the "good girl" image, I know you're interested. I'll be here when you want to experience a real man."

I thought about the incident all evening, and was so upset, I contemplated a job change as soon as possible. Though I wanted to talk to someone, I was afraid to utter a word. Fortunately, Lucas came to town the next day and we went for a drive in the hills. I felt I could safely confide my frustrations to him.

"Sara, I want you out of there. If you stay, there's likely to be a killing, if not by Mitch, then possibly by me."

I patted his chest. "I didn't mean to upset you, Lucas. Believe me, I've done nothing to give Steven the wrong idea. I love my job, but it's become very uncomfortable."

"The nerve of that bastard! He knows you're a sweet girl, and that's why he's preying on you. I'd like to punch him in the head."

I sighed. "I really don't want a scene. There's no sense in innocent people being hurt."

"Like who?"

"His family."

"That would be unfortunate, but he deserves it, Sara."

I decided to change the subject. "Thanks for listening, Lucas. Hopefully, I'll find another job soon."

"I might have an idea," Lucas pondered. "I'll make a phone call tomorrow."

We drove to The Foxhole. Lucas saddled up to the bar, and I joined Gunner in his office. We sorted through stacks of Xeroxed materials and put together a promotional flier. After setting the food and drink specials, we scheduled the bands for each night. Gunner looked down the hall and pointed to Lucas, who chatted with Pete. "Did you guys come in together?" he asked.

"Yeah."

"Something going on?"

I couldn't resist. "With Lucas and Pete?"

He gave me a sideways look. "You're such a bullshitter."

"Growing up with you and Mitch, I came by it honest."

He agreed. "That's the damned truth. Come on, I need to talk to Lucas. I might need his help later tonight."

As Gunner and I approached the bar, an obviously intoxicated blonde jumped on the stool beside Lucas. She tapped his shoulder, then gave his bicep a squeeze. "*Ooohhh!* You're so hard. I love muscles. Wanna' dance with me?"

Lucas leaned back a little.

A sudden possessiveness came over me. I bolted over, wedged my body between them, and threw my arms around Lucas' neck. "Take me home, baby," I cooed.

I felt a tap on my shoulder. "Hey wait a minute. I saw him first."

I gave the blonde my cattiest expression. "Buzz off; he's taken."

She muttered under her breath and staggered away.

Gunner stared at me. "I'm not even going to ask what you're up to," he said before turning his attention to Lucas. "Will you meet up with me and Mitch at closing time? I'll explain then."

Lucas nodded. "Sure thing, brother."

Gunner teased me, "I hope that's okay with you?"

Lucas and I headed outside. I couldn't help but ask. "I wonder what's up?"

"I'm wondering myself," he answered.

"Maybe help with some heavy lifting?"

Lucas stopped in his tracks. "Wait a minute. You're talking about Gunner?"

"Who did you think I was talking about? The blonde? You need to stay away from her. She's dangerous, and it's a good thing I had your back."

He tried to get a rise from me. "Had my back? You just blew my hot date."

I whirled to face him, hands on my hips. "Hey, you're supposed to be hanging out with me today. But if she's more your type, I'll go grab her for you."

He pretended to think it over, then laughed and wrapped an arm around my shoulder. "Dammit girl, you know better."

He started his truck. "Are you busy tomorrow night?" he asked shyly.

"Lucas, my entire calendar is open while you're in town."

He grinned. "The county fair is going on. Remember the school field trips? I thought it would be fun to go again, like old times?"

"Oh my gosh, yes. Who all is going?"

He leaned closer, "I was thinking just you and me, if that's alright?"

As a child, I'd looked forward to the fair all year long. Thoughts of it still made me giddy with excitement. "Let's do it. I can't wait. Pick me up after work."

The following day couldn't pass quickly enough. The weather was clear, cool, and perfect. After months of work and classes, I was ready for a little fun. I pulled on my newest jeans, and choose a white tank top to wear under a soft flannel shirt. Lucas picked me up after work. As he drove, he filled me in on the shenanigans from the previous night.

Recently, while Pete was on duty at The Foxhole, his new lawnmower went missing. It was nothing fancy, just the push kind. Pete told Gunner, that on the day he brought it home from the store, his neighbors from down the road drove by, just as he was unloading it. Known to be a bunch of thugs, Pete was ninety-nine percent sure that they were the culprits who stole it. So, Gunner suggested a plan to sneak over to the neighbor's place for a little peek.

At two a.m., as Pete cleaned the bar, Gunner, Mitch, and Lucas left together. Mitch drove his pickup, as they passed by Pete's neighbor's house very slowly. All the lights were off, with the exception of a porch light in the back. They were obviously asleep. Mitch parked his truck out of sight and the three of them snuck to the fence. Gunner opened the gate and took a bundle of beef jerky from his pocket. He and the yard dog made friends really quick. Lucas pointed to a storage building in the back yard, partially lit by the porch light. They moved closer to the building, and it appeared to have only one door. Problem was, a fence was built around it; a fence holding several large pigs. Gunner had laid out the plans earlier, Lucas was to keep watch, using their secret bird call to warn of trouble.

Lucas took his post between the house and the pen. Gunner made a signal to Mitch, and they split up. Gunner headed to the back of the building, while Mitch jumped the fence, and made his way through the muddy lot, carefully stepping around the lounging pigs. Once Mitch made it to the storage building, he grabbed for the door knob. At the same moment, Gunner opened the door from the inside, sending Mitch into a panic. He jumped backwards, and his feet slid out from under him. Gunner cussed, as mayhem set in. The pigs jumped to their feet, and ran wildly around. A few of them stepped on Mitch as he lay on the ground.

Lucas, consumed with laughter, could barely stand. Gunner gestured for Mitch to get up and follow him inside the building, where they found the mower, covered with a tarp. The two of them carried the mower through the pig lot, and back to Mitch's truck—miraculously without being shot at.

I shook my head as the tale ended. "So, I'm assuming the ride back home with Mitch was rather unpleasant?"

"Whew, you got that right," Lucas said. "Actually, we made him ride in the back of his own pickup."

I smiled. "Sounds like old times."

He patted my thigh. "Yeah, I couldn't wait to tell you."

When we arrived at the fairgrounds, Lucas pulled into a parking spot and killed the motor. This was as good a time as any, I thought. "Speaking of Mitch, how is he?" I asked.

He unbuckled his seat belt and rubbed the back of his neck.

My throat tightened. "Paulette said he's…"

"Using meth?"

I sighed. "Yeah."

"He's never used in front of me, but I've heard talk, and suspected it for a while. So has Gunner, and he's fed up. Even threatened to fire Mitch."

I felt like my heart had been ripped out. "Is this why Val left him?"

Lucas shrugged. "My guess is she finally caught on."

Things were still unclear. "How did he get involved with this stuff?"

Lucas leaned across the steering wheel. "To my knowledge, he never used until he went to work at The Foxhole. And the last thing Gunner needs is a bad reputation for the bar. I believe Gunner feels responsible somehow. They talked, but Mitch denied it. Sara, he knows better than to get involved with shit like this. Honestly. I'd like to put my boot up his ass."

It was almost more than I could absorb. I blinked back tears and scooted closer.

"Thanks for being honest with me. Things are a little clearer now. I wish there was something I could do to help him."

"We all want to help him. Hopefully, he'll see the light soon." Lucas cupped the sides of my face in his hands. "Enough of this seriousness, let's go have some fun."

The rides were in full swing, a blur of neon lights zipped up, down and around the sky. After a dare to get on the scariest ride with him, Lucas bought us sodas and corn dogs. He pointed toward the livestock barn. "Let's go over there."

Someone yelled out his name; a teenaged boy in a cowboy hat.

"That's Joey Miller's little brother, Cletus." Lucas said.

We walked to the stall where Cletus prepared his hog for its judging.

"That's a nice one," Lucas said. "Good luck."

Cletus reached to shake Lucas's hand. "Thanks. Joey said you live Wyoming now. Your girlfriend is pretty."

Lucas nodded. "Yep, just in town for a few days. This is Sara Ryan. Sara, meet Cletus, who's trying to steal you away, I believe?"

I laughed as Cletus tipped his hat.

"Is Joey still chasing the rodeo circuit?" Lucas asked.

"Yeah, he's riding bulls."

Just then, several of Cletus's belt-buckled friends approached.

"Play That Funky Music" by Wild Cherry erupted on the overhead speakers. Lucas let out a howl, dipped his knees, and swayed slightly to the beat. Right then and there, the cowboys broke into their best dance moves, competing to out-do one another.

"Look out!" Lucas warned as someone's pig made a break for it.

Lucas pulled me from its path, and the young cowboys chased behind it. "Happens every time." he said. "Ready for cotton candy?"

I gripped his arm, "I'm not leaving here without it."

I stood back while Lucas waited in the concession line. Three high school girls were checking him out discreetly, or so they thought. Dressed as he was, in a snap-up western shirt, Wrangler jeans, and a baseball cap worn backwards, he had my attention, too. The girls elbowed one another as he walked past them with our cotton candy. I giggled when they discovered that I was watching them. Lucas spun around to see what was so funny.

I teased him, "You're certainly stirring up all the girls tonight."

We strolled back to his truck, and he lowered the tailgate. While we sat, like a gentleman, he hand-fed me the sugary strands so my fingers wouldn't get sticky. Occasionally, he enjoyed a bite for himself. I leaned back on my elbows to admire the harvest moon.

I pointed as a jet crossed the sky. "Do you ever wonder about the people on planes? Like, who they are and where they're going?"

He looked up; his honey-colored skin glowed under the moonlight. He shook his head. "No, not really. My interests are focused on the girl in front of me."

A warmth crept over me. I sat up, took a slow breath and exhaled. If I crossed the line, things might never be the same between us again. Was it worth the risk? Something stirred in my core, a soft fluttering. Without a doubt, it was butterflies, and I could no longer ignore them.

I grabbed his shirt collar and pulled him close to my face. I closed my eyes and breathed him in, faint hints of soap and cologne. Lucas didn't waste the opportunity. He brushed the tip of his nose to mine, then kissed me softly. Once, and then again. Intoxicated with desire, I opened my eyes to seek his reaction.

He whispered. "I've waited so long."

I let him kiss me again; harder, and desperately. I felt so secure in his arms. But, like a flash, my doubts appeared from nowhere and I released my grip and pulled away from him.

What if this was a mistake, I wondered? Unable to look him in the eyes, I slid off the tailgate and stammered. "I'm sorry. I...I don't know what came over me. I didn't mean to be so forward."

He touched my shoulder. "You don't owe me an apology. Honestly, it's probably the best thing that's ever happened to me."

I toyed with a strand of my hair. "I'm ready to go if you are?"

As he drove me home, I was frozen in panic. I feared Lucas would have expectations of me. He was quiet, but glanced over at me occasionally. He parked outside my house and reached for his door handle.

"It's okay." I blurted out. "You don't have to walk me. I'll talk to you tomorrow, okay?"

I could hear the disappointment in his "goodnight."

I kept my conversations with Lucas light and casual until he left for Wyoming. Soon after, I confided my situation to Grandma Janie.

"There's nothing wrong with taking your time," she advised. "Don't rush your feelings. Let them flow naturally."

The fall air turned cooler, as the squirrels in Grandma's yard scrambled for nuts—a prediction of an early winter. It was my turn to do her shopping, so I rose early on Saturday morning and went to collect her list. When I got to her place, she was in the recliner with a blanket draped around her shoulders.

"Have you had your coffee yet?" I asked.

She nodded. "Yes, but it didn't seem to do the trick. May I ask a favor? Would you drop something off to Mitch?"

"Sure, what do you have for him?"

She pointed to the kitchen table. "A plate of brownies. He hasn't been by in some time now. I miss him."

I drove to his house, but his pickup was gone. No big deal, I thought. I'd come back on my return trip. But when I passed The Foxhole, I saw his truck under a large tree by the parking lot. I turned in and got out of my Jeep. When I peered into his pickup, I found him asleep on the seat. I quietly turned to leave, then changed my mind. How dare he avoid our grandma for so long? I went back and pulled on the door handle, but it was locked. I tapped lightly on the window. "Mitch?

He lifted his head and waved me on, "Not now."

I argued, "I can't leave you here. Come on, open up."

He shielded his eyes with his forearm. "I said, not now."

My temper flared. "Not now, my ass! Are you so messed up you can't talk to me?"

Mitch growled, "Get out of here."

I jumped back, surprised by his abrasiveness. "I'll tell you what, Mitch. Our Grandmother misses you so much, she sent a plate of brownies for you. Is there some reason you can't make time to see her anymore?"

He bolted up in the seat and opened the door. "Would you please get off my back?" He put both of his bare feet on the ground, but had to hold the door to steady himself.

I ordered him, "Get in my Jeep, I'll take you home."

He held the plate of brownies as I drove. After a few yawns, he attempted to make small talk. "So, how've you been?"

"Worried about you."

He made light of the situation. "No need to be. I had a little too much last night, that's all."

I stopped in his driveway, but I couldn't let it go. "My Lord, are you that far gone? You look like hammered shit. Not only that, you stink."

"That's enough!"

I lowered my tone, and attempted to get through his thick skull. "You still have a good job at the mill, if you'll just quit the bar and all this other bull—"

He interrupted, "You don't know a thing."

Tears began to sting my eyes. "You might take me for a fool, but I know what you're doing."

"Just shut up!" he yelled. "I want you to stay out of this."

He jumped out and flung the plate. The brownies flew out from under the plastic wrap and landed on the floorboard. I cried and pounded the horn on my steering wheel. He walked away and didn't bother looking back.

THREE

The Darkness

Two weeks had passed since my argument with Mitch. I decided it was best to put distance between myself and my cousins. After all, I had enough to concentrate on, like college classes and my job. I tried not to think about Mitch or his issues, yet every time I drove by The Foxhole—which was every day—my resentment grew.

At work, things were tense with Steven, and he seemed to go out of his way to make me feel uncomfortable. Still insulted by my rejection, no doubt. He was often moody and sullen, and only spoke to me when necessary.

It was Monday of Thanksgiving week. When I came home from work, Momma said I had missed a call from Lucas. An hour later, he called back to tell me that his cousin Carl, a pharmacist in Tahlequah, was interested in hiring additional help. He gave me a phone number, and instructed me to call the pharmacy as soon as possible. I thanked him and made small talk, purposely keeping our conversation brief. Although I owed Lucas an explanation for my recent behavior, I hadn't summed up my feelings just yet.

The next day, I dialed the number to City Pharmacy. Rhonda--one of the aides, took my call, and asked if I could come in on Wednesday at ten a.m. I accepted the appointment, hung up the phone, and flung my closet door open in a panic. What on Earth was I going to wear for the interview? After a consult with Momma, we put together an outfit that was conservative, yet young. I slept very little that night, and tossed and turned with anticipation.

After my drive into Tahlequah, I parked in front of an old, two-story brick building. The bell on the door jingled as I walked through. I went up to the counter and checked in with Rhonda, who handed me an application and an ink pen, then showed me to a chair. That's when my nervousness went into high gear. I filled out the application, then ten minutes later, Rhonda re-appeared. "Carl will see you now. Follow me."

Rhonda led me to an office in the back and opened the door. I stepped inside to find a beautiful, raven-haired woman sitting at a mahogany desk. She stood and offered her hand. "Sara, how nice to meet you."

I was taken aback. "It's nice to meet you…Carl?"

She laughed. "I get that a lot. My given name is Carlotta, but the family calls me Carl. Please sit."

I handed her my application, and after a brief review, she flipped it over and pushed it aside. "Listen, I don't feel the need to ask for references. Lucas has answered most of my questions already. He gave you a glowing recommendation, by the way. We'll make this quick, okay?"

I nodded. My nerves began to settle. Carl asked me to describe my current duties for Steven, and she inquired about my career interests. At the end of the interview, she briefed me on her background, and told me of her future plans to expand the pharmacy. She spoke of her goals, like making medicine more accessible to all of the community, particularly the elderly and low-incomed.

Carl put both elbows on the desk and pressed her palms together. "Lucas and I speak once or twice each month. He gets pretty lonely up there in Wyoming. He thinks very highly of you and your family, Sara."

I smiled. "Likewise."

"Well, I've made my decision. I'd love to have you here. Can you start in two weeks?"

We negotiated a wage agreement, considerably more than my current one. I left there on Cloud Nine, and to celebrate, I drove to Dairy Queen for a chocolate shake. I opted for the back roads on the way back to Waya, and rolled down my window to enjoy the fresh aroma of the countryside. As I cruised along, I noticed a farm that rendered the picture-perfect image of Oklahoma. Bison and cattle grazed the rolling hills. The land was dotted with black oil wells, which resembled crows pecking away at the ground. Scissortail Flycatchers zipped playfully over the tall Indian grass as it swayed in the breeze. I drove upon an enormous red barn, just as an Appaloosa emerged with her young colt. I was taken with their beauty, and stepped on the brake to watch for a moment. The pair stared at me briefly, then went on about their day.

On my way again, I could barely contain my excitement, and looked forward to sharing the news with everyone. I whispered a prayer of thanks. How eager I was to begin my new job, but would have to serve a two weeks' notice first. Although I dreaded his initial reaction, I hoped Steven would eventually be happy for me.

The next morning, I crossed the Main Street Pharmacy parking lot with newfound confidence. I walked in the door as Steven completed a customer consult. Once in the break room, I grabbed a cup of coffee. Within moments, I heard the rustle of his heavily starched lab coat, as he made his way down the hall.

Steven acknowledged me with an obligatory hello, then asked about my day off.

"It was great, actually," I said. My hands grew sweaty as I clenched my letter of notice. "Steven, can we talk for a minute?"

He pulled a chair out for me, and then placed a foot on the one next to it. He leaned on a knee and faced me. I swallowed hard and placed the paper on the table in front of him.

"What's this?" He swiped the notice off the table, scanned it, then threw it across the room. "So, just like that, you're walking out on me?"

I hadn't expected this much anger.

"Do you realize what I could have given you someday?" he said.

I tried to reason with him. "Steven, as I said in my notice, I'm willing to thoroughly train my replacement..."

"I don't need you!" He marched away, then stomped back in the room with a checkbook. He opened it and scribbled out a check, then pushed it forcefully at the center of my chest. I clutched it by reflex.

He slammed the checkbook closed and began to rant. 'That should cover your time here. Feel free to leave now."

My cheeks stung with anger. In my opinion, I'd been a stellar employee. What gave him the right to treat me this way? I wasn't going to take it. "You're only mad because you failed to get me in bed."

He turned his back. "Wait and see…One day you'll realize how badly you've fucked up. Have a nice life, Sara."

I laughed and grabbed my purse. "Whatever, pervert. And by the way, I'll have a fabulous life, no thanks to you."

I didn't let the door hit my butt on the way out. I drove straight to the bank, deposited my check, then hurried to Grandma's house. I found her reclined in front of the television, watching a soap opera with a glass of iced tea in her hand. I waited for a commercial break, then filled her in on my morning. She shook her head and called Steven a scoundrel under her breath.

"With a great career, a family, money and everything, why isn't he satisfied, Grandma?"

She shrugged. "Do you remember the legend about Coyote and the Star?"

I thought back. "Only bits and pieces."

Grandma ignored her tv show long enough to refresh me on the old tale.

"The Great Spirit had favored Coyote with good medicine--so much, that Coyote began to feel very powerful. He was convinced that he had more power than the Great Spirit himself.

One night, as Coyote sat atop the highest mountain, he gazed upon a brilliant star that stood out in the heavens. He howled, "Come to me, beautiful Star. I wish to dance with you."

Star descended low enough for Coyote to take hold of her. Then, she soared to the most amazing heights with him in tow. He clung to her for dear life as she whisked him round and round the universe. Despite Coyote's deep fascination with her, he soon became tired and struggled to hold on.

"Star," he pled, "I've danced with you long enough. I'm going to let go and head back home now."

"No, wait!" Star warned, clutching him tightly. "We're too high. I'll take you back to your mountain soon."

But Coyote grew impatient and wished to have his way. He let go of her, despite her wishes, and began to fall so fast that when he hit the Earth, his body flattened out like a pancake. Once he came to, he opened his eyes to see that the paw he had held onto Star with was missing. Desperate for help, he hobbled to The Great Spirit.

"Great Spirit, will you help me get my paw back from Star?" he asked. "How will I be able to hunt without it?"

The Great Spirit spoke. "Foolish Coyote, you believed you could do supernatural things and come out unscathed? Now you must wait until Star returns. Only then will you get your paw back."

Coyote was relieved. His ears perked up. "That is good news. But how long will I have to wait for her?"

The Great Spirit answered. "Oh, that will require some patience, you see. She will not return for several Moons."

I listened to Grandma's words, still a little unsure. "So, it was greed that crippled him?"

She shrugged. "People dance with many things: greed, lust, addiction. Each comes with a hefty price tag."

My thoughts suddenly turned to Mitch, though I hesitated to mention it. "Grandma, I'm worried about Mitch." Guilt crept over me, just like years ago when I tattled on him for throwing rocks at her chickens.

She showed no surprise. "He's on dope, I assume?"

I couldn't lie to her. "That's what I've heard."

She stood and picked up her glass. "He's in the Devil's grip, which is why he avoids me, just as his mother did. Regardless, I'll do what I can to help him."

I shook my head. "I'm afraid he won't listen to you, much less anyone else."

She held up her hand to silence me. "I know, I've lived this before. But I'll do my best to deal with him. In the meanwhile, you must pray for him, Sara. Sometimes that's the most we can offer."

I woke before 7 a.m. on Thanksgiving Day, and rolled over in bed to look out the window. Grandma and I had been up late baking pies, so I'd slept over. A cold draft filtered through the windowsill. The sun peeped across the frosted field, and the weathervane battled a wicked north wind. I pulled a thick blanket up to cover my nose, before the sudden clatter of pots and pans startled me. Familiar voices came from the kitchen; it was Mom and Aunt Katie, who arrived early to prepare our holiday meal. I sat up in bed to eavesdrop.

"James said Mitch's job at the mill is on thin ice," Momma said. "He can't seem to clock in on time. That is, when he actually shows up to work."

Aunt Katie chimed in, "He needs to straighten up, and Gunner agrees. If Mitch knows what's best for him, he'll hold onto his mill job. Good jobs don't grow on trees around here."

My Mom whispered, "If the rumors are true that he's on dope, it'll break Momma's heart. Especially after what happened to Julia."

"Yes, it will break all of our hearts," Aunt Katie said. "He's been so out of touch lately; I wonder if he'll even show up today. Maybe one of us should call and remind him about dinner."

I pulled on my socks and robe, then sneaked up on them. "You aren't being as quiet as you think," I said. "I heard every word of your conversation."

Aunt Katie kissed my forehead. "Sorry to wake you, baby. Let me pour you a cup of coffee."

Grandma Janie flew in under the radar, too. Most likely, she had overheard the conversation as well. "Good morning, girls," she said, then poured a cup of coffee and added a splash of cream. She ambled over to her cupboard, choose a variety of spices, and organized them on the countertop. She sipped her coffee and peered out a window. "There's definitely frost on the pumpkins this morning." She turned to face us, "I suppose you want me to make the dressing?"

"Please." I said, since hers was the best.

"Just as I thought. I'll get started right after my coffee. I assume everyone will be here for dinner? Sara, please give Mitch a call to remind him."

"Yes, ma'am." I answered. Not exactly the task I'd hoped for.

A couple hours later, I put on makeup and got dressed. Grandma's house was lively on holidays, especially Thanksgiving. The men were gathered around a football game on tv, while in the kitchen, a Dean Martin record spun on an old record player. Sometimes Mom and Aunt Katie stopped cooking long enough to swing their hips to the music.

I went to the phone and dialed Mitch's number. He answered on the sixth ring, his voice hoarse and groggy.

"Gobble, gobble," I said.

His chuckle sounded forced.

"Sorry to wake you, but I'm only following orders. Grandma is expecting you for dinner. Will you be here?"

He spoke through a yawn. "Sure, I'll be over in a bit."

Our conversation went better than I expected. Just as I hung up, Gunner arrived with Uncle Ted. I opened the door to let them in. My great-uncle walked straight to the heater in the corner of the living room. "Osiyo. Whew, it's cold this morning! Gotta' warm these hands up, sis."

Gunner lagged behind, and had just reached the porch steps. I walked outside to greet him. He stopped, and reached for my steaming cup of coffee.

"When did you start drinking this stuff?" he asked, then took a cautious sip.

"Years ago," I answered.

"This wind gives 'cold as a witch's tit' a whole new meaning, doesn't it? I heard you got a new job. Congratulations."

I smiled. "Thank you. I can't wait to start."

"I remember when Carl and her parents used to visit Lucas's family. What a great gal. Is she single?" he asked.

I shrugged. "I'm not sure. You should ask Lucas when he gets here. Oh, by the way, I called Mitch and he said he'll be along soon."

Gunner eyed me suspiciously. "I'm a little surprised to hear that, considering the shape he was in just a few hours ago."

"I hope he's okay," I said.

I wanted to ask questions, but recalled Mitch's demand that I butt out.

Gunner sat on the porch railing and stared at the floor. "You know, I really wish I knew how to answer that. He'd better hold onto his real job, because his days are numbered at The Foxhole."

All bets were off now. I dove in head first. "Really? What happened? Are you planning to fire him?"

"If it were entirely up to me, I would have done it already. That's all I can tell you."

Gunner wanted to leave the conversation there, but I took the chance. "So, you're saying if Mitch no longer works at the bar, things will run better for you somehow?

Gunner sighed. "Sly as a fox. How do I get myself into these conversations with you?"

Little did he know, I was just getting started. "Seriously, what is the benefit of firing Mitch?"

He hesitated, then rubbed his forehead. "I don't expect you to understand, Sara."

I continued to push my luck.

"Well, why don't you try me?"

He stood and stepped closer. "Dammit. I assume you know about his meth problem? Everyone else does. Clear enough? Let's change the subject, okay?"

"What does that have to do with The Foxhole?"

Gunner handed me the now empty cup. "For fuck's sake, he's made some stupid mistakes. He's a liability."

I cringed. "I can't believe my ears. How did he get mixed up in all of this?"

It killed me to think of Mitch putting poison in his body. And what about Lance and Chester? Were they involved? My concerns grew greater by the minute.

Gunner's patience wore thin. "Oh, good Lord, what have I started here? To be honest, he started using meth just a couple times a week, like when he worked late at the bar. Ya' know, just to give him some energy. Then it turned into a daily habit. I tried to help him, believe me, but he claimed he had everything under control. This is of his own doing, Sara."

I crossed my arms. "The meth…It must be convenient to come by?"

He squinted, then hovered over me. "What are you getting at?"

"You must know who supplies him? Therefore, you could have done something about it, right?"

He glared. "Am I wrong, or was that an accusation?"

I looked Gunner in the eye. "Why didn't you stop him? We're supposed to watch out for one another, remember? We're each other's keepers."

"You're upset with me because *he's* irresponsible? Don't get me wrong, Sara. I realize what a rough life Mitch has had, but I refuse to carry the blame for his situation. He had a great wife, and he blew it. And now, he's in danger of losing not one, but both of his jobs. I gave him a chance to make extra money, and how does he thank me? By getting an addiction and causing problems at The Foxhole."

I tried to rein in my emotions, but a tear spilled down my cheek. "Is this drug activity tied to the bar?"

Gunner snapped. "How dare you even *think* I'm running a shady operation! And you, of all people, know that Mitch is like a brother to me."

I could tell that Gunner was being straight up, then I suddenly felt like the biggest jerk in town. I'd been taught better than to take sides between my cousins. Where was Lucas—our mediator—when I needed him?

I placed a hand on Gunner's heart. "I'm sorry for misjudging you. Please forgive me?"

He covered my hand with his and squeezed softly. "I know it's a mess right now, but everything will get better. Until then, I want you to chill out. Concentrate on your own stuff, okay?"

It was Gunner's polite way of asking me to butt out.

We watched as Mitch's truck pulled onto Blackberry Lane. Gunner gestured toward the house. "Go on inside. I want to talk to him privately." Gunner smiled as I walked away, "Don't worry. I'm not mad at you."

I returned inside, but spied on them from a window. Mitch squinted through a swollen eye. He waved his hands around as if trying to explain himself. Things seemed heated between them. Gunner's cheeks turned red, and he held a finger close to Mitch's face.

That's when Uncle Ted approached me. "What's going on out there?" I stepped away from the window. Ted looked for himself. "Uh oh," he said.

Uncle Ted stepped onto the porch. "Hey, now!"

My cousins whirled around in surprise.

"Aren't you guys cold? Come on in. It's almost time to eat."

Uncle Ted and I stood in the doorway as Gunner and Mitch filed past us. Mitch appeared nervous and ill at ease.

I stalled the crowd. "Wait, is Lucas with his parents, or is he eating with us?"

"He won't be here today." Mitch answered in passing.

I grabbed his coat sleeve. "What do you mean?"

"He stayed in Wyoming."

My heart sank. "But that's not like him. He's always home for the holidays."

Mitch shrugged. "He's working two jobs. Maybe that's why."

He and Gunner looked at me, puzzled by my concern. I followed them to the table, but my appetite was gone. Once seated, we all joined hands before Grandma said Grace. "Dear Lord, we thank you for the togetherness we share, for our good health, and the delicious food before us..."

The funny thing about adulthood is how months fly by, like leaves in the wind. It was February, and my family hadn't come together since the holidays. I'd completed training for my new job, and found Carl to be patient and helpful. Due to a much lower stress level, I was motivated, and my grades were better than ever.

Despite hectic schedules, Gillie and I did our best to stay in touch. She had taken a receptionist job for a local dentist back in November, and met an interesting young man on her very first day. "Jay Bob" came into the office with an aching wisdom tooth, which required surgery. When he came back for a follow-up appointment, he presented Gillie with a rose, and thanked her for her post-op phone call. It was his perfect opportunity to slip her a note:

"Roses are red, violets are blue, the swelling is down, so now I can chew. Will you go to dinner with me?"

She accepted. It wasn't long before Jay Bob took priority with Gillie's free time. It seemed as if our plans to attend college together were gone. But, seeing her so happy gave me joy, and I eventually came to terms with my disappointment.

One Saturday morning, she caught me at home long enough for a phone chat. I'll never forget her call. I was propped up in bed with coffee and a *"Rolling Stone"* magazine when she rang. As soon as I answered, she blurted out, "You're not going to believe this…I'm engaged!"

I was speechless, but she barely noticed. "Sara, I'm getting married. Will you be my maid of honor?"

Tears rushed to my eyes. "Oh my gosh! Yes, yes, of course. Tell me more."

"Well, we went for a walk yesterday at Jay Bob's parent's place. We were by the pond, and he dropped to one knee and pulled a ring out of his shirt pocket. I was in shock, but I said yes."

I stood up and began to pace around my bedroom.

"Wow, I can't believe this," I admitted. "It seems to have happened so fast."

"I know, but I really love him. I was so excited; I didn't sleep a wink last night. What do you think of the colors aqua and ivory?"

"I know you love him, and yes— yes, that sounds beautiful. So, when's the big event?"

She was in her typical chatterbox mode, and only came up for air every now and then. "This June, so make sure Lucas is in town. I added him to the guest list."

"You've already made the guest list?" I asked.

Gillie sighed. "Sara, you know how I am."

I tried not to laugh. "Okay, I'll make sure to tell Lucas, though unfortunately we don't talk much anymore."

You could have heard a pin drop.

"Seriously? Did he finally take the hint that you're not interested?"

I sulked. "I suppose, but now I feel shitty. He probably thinks I led him on."

Her voice grew serious. "Sara, I'm sure you're relieved. But it sounds like you miss him a little. Do you?"

I decided to come clean. "Maybe? I mean, there's like a void in my life now. I miss his voice, his laugh…Everything. I'm so confused."

"Sounds like a yes to me."

I could almost hear her smile. I plopped down on the bed. "Okay, yes. Either that or an extreme case of loneliness on my part."

"Well, you should do something about it and tell him."

I was quick with an excuse. "He's probably dating someone else."

"Just be honest with him. I bet he'll come running."

I gazed up at the Roger Daltrey poster on my ceiling. "Oh God, why am I suddenly so nervous? Enough about my problems. Shouldn't we be planning your wedding?"

"Girl, I'll need help, so expect to be seeing a lot more of me," she promised.

The thought made me happy. Before hanging up, she made a request. "Please call Lucas tonight. I'll expect a full report tomorrow."

I spent the rest of the day deep in thought. My anxiety must have been obvious as I hurried through supper.

"Everything okay, baby?" my dad asked.

I looked at him, and then to my mom. "Yes, why?"

"Well, you've looked up at the wall clock about eight times in the past fifteen minutes."

Mom joined the interrogation. "Are you going out tonight?"

"No, I'm going to study after I call Lucas."

"You haven't mentioned him lately," Mom said.

"Oh, he's fine, I'm sure." I took my plate and fork to the sink.

Dad filled Mom in. "Lucas is one hardworking kid. Gunner said he's a construction worker during the week and a ranch hand on weekends."

Mom nodded. "Well, that would explain why we haven't seen him in months. It's very unusual for him to stay away for this long."

"He's trying to save up some money," I said. "He has goals."

Dad piped in. "Yeah, the horse-training outfit, right?"

"What?" Mom asked. "When is this happening? And where?"

I leaned back against the counter and gave Dad the floor.

"Gunner said Lucas wants to move back here soon," he said.

"Well, I'm happy for him," Mom said. "Sara, please tell him hello for us."

I nodded. "Oh, I almost forgot, Gillie's engaged. She asked me to be her maid of honor."

There was a brief silence.

Finally, Dad spoke. "Engaged? Why, she's just a baby!"

"Well, she's an adult now, James. So is our daughter." Mom winked at me.

Dad shook his head in disbelief. "I don't believe I'm ready for all this."

Once in my bedroom, I took a deep breath and dialed Lucas's number. After a few rings, he answered, but seemed surprised to hear from me. He immediately asked if something was wrong.

I laughed. "You think something's wrong because I called you?"

"Well, that was my first thought," he admitted.

I wasn't sure he was happy to hear from me. "You sound tired. Did I wake you?"

"I drifted off watching tv," he yawned.

I bit my lip in suspense. "I heard you've been working really hard. Is that why you haven't visited lately?"

His reply was short and sweet. "Yeah, pretty much."

My apprehensions ran wild. Should I approach this gently, or just spill it? I held my breath, and my mouth went dry. "Because of me?"

He hesitated. "No, don't worry about it. We're good."

I could always read between his lines, and something wasn't right. I fidgeted with the phone cord. "I'd like to try to explain something, if you'll just hear me out?"

"Explain what?"

"My behavior that night at the fair. I'm sure it confused you. Sometimes I second-guess my feelings, and then panic sets in. But, now that I've sorted things out, something is very clear to me; I miss you, your laugh, your voice, and your hugs. And although I can't predict what the future holds, I want you to know that I really care about you."

"Thank you," he said politely. "I'm glad to hear it."

"You're welcome. And, if umm, I mean, what I'm trying to say is…"

"Go ahead."

"If you're still interested, I'd like to get to know you better, one-on-one. Like I said, if you're still interested?"

His voice soothed me. "I never intended to pressure you at all."

My heart was racing. "No, no, of course not. It was all me. I panicked and I'm so sorry about that."

"Well, we'll just take our time and see where this goes," he said. "Which won't be difficult since I live in Wyoming."

I sighed, now at-ease. "When are you coming home again?"

"You said you've missed me?" he asked. His lazy drawl stirred my sleeping butterflies.

"You have no idea," I answered.

He chuckled a little. "Well, in that case, I'll see you next month."

I was on my way to Grandma's house a week later, when I met Mitch on the road. He waved and motioned me over. I quickly pulled into the church parking lot, and watched him turn his pickup around. It was a chilly gray day, the clouds hung dark and low. He left his truck and walked over. "Busy?" he asked.

"I'm on my way to see Grandma. What's up?"

He scanned the sky above us. "Are we under a tornado warning?"

I rolled my eyes.

"Got time for a ride first?" he asked.

"Sure," I said, wondering what this was about.

He jumped in. "Let's go to the river crossing."

Hopefully he doesn't intend to drown me, I wondered? He said very little on the five-mile ride. We listened to the radio instead. *"Melissa"* by the Allman Brothers Band came on. The moment I parked; Mitch was out the door. "Let's walk," he suggested.

His appearance was gaunt, and he seemed to have lost weight since Thanksgiving. My heart sank as I followed him to the water's edge. He picked up a stone and skipped it all the way to the opposite shore.

"Pretty good," I said. So, he did it again.

"Lucas called the other night. He mentioned that the two of you might start dating. I assume he wanted my approval. Why didn't you tell me?"

I laughed it off. "I didn't realize it would be a big deal to anyone."

Mitch's tone changed from carefree to critical. "Yeah, it's a big deal. It's weird, I mean, he's like a brother, and now he's…"

I interrupted him. "Don't put the cart before the horse, okay?"

He looked in my eyes. "Well, it's inevitable, isn't it?"

I was a bit shocked by his reaction. "Thoughts of me with Lucas bother you? But you've always respected him."

"Only some thoughts, not all of them."

"Is this you being protective, or is something else going on here?" I asked.

He sat on the cold rocks. His hands trembled. After a bit of silence, he spoke, while staring into the distance. "I don't like having these thoughts. I wish I could explain it."

It was suddenly clear to me. Since birth, my cousins and I were taught to love one another. But there are many types of love: innocent, passionate, brotherly, forbidden. And once under love's spell, lines become blurred, and caution is thrown to the wind. We ignore the taboos and stay in the shadows, where we dance until the shame disappears.

I dropped to my knees and wrapped my arms around his shoulders. "I'd be a hypocrite to say I don't understand. Now you know why I always resented your girl-friends. I worried that if you gave them your love, there wouldn't be any left for me." With my cheek pressed to his, we were dangerously close. "But I came to realize that we're always connected…Until we die, and even beyond. You'll never lose me, Mitch. No matter who, no matter what."

He reached to touch my face. "You're all I've got in this world," he said.

"That's not true. Others care, if you'll just let them."

We huddled together as darkness fell.

"We should go back to the Jeep," I said. "It's freezing out here."

"In a few minutes. I want to tell you what happened after everyone left on Thanksgiving Day. Uncle Ted and Grandma gave me a stern talking-to. I've never been so ashamed in my life."

"Worse than when Grandma caught you and Gunner smoking in the cellar?"

He chuckled. "Damn, I'd almost forgotten about that. And yeah, much worse. Uncle Ted said, 'You can't just dip your toe in the Devil's Lake or you'll soon be swimming in it.' Then they led me to the backyard and put me through the protection ritual. You know-- the one where they light tobacco and pray over you?"

I nodded. "They did it for Gunner before he went to Vietnam."

"Gunner came home alive," Mitch said. "But I'm my own worst enemy."

I had no words, but pointed to the crescent Moon hanging over the horizon.

Mitch stood and extended a hand to help me up. "Don't worry, Sara. I'll get it figured out. Might even make you proud of me again."

I gave him a nod, and we walked away from the river. Once we arrived back to the church, Mitch opened the door and smiled over his shoulder. "Weird or not, you've got my approval. I know Lucas will be good to you."

I arrived at Grandma's house and she asked me to sit at the kitchen table. "Want some hot cocoa?"

"Please." My hands were still cold from being at the crossing. Grandma spoke as she made our cocoa on the stovetop. "I was thinking, since Ted's seventieth birthday is next weekend, we should throw him a surprise party. Are you available to help?"

"Of course," I said. "Do you want to have it here?"

"No, he hasn't felt like getting out lately, so we should go to his place. He'll be more comfortable there. Since Katie and Anna have been cleaning house for him, I'll have them go over and tidy things up." Grandma said.

"Okay, so what would you like for me to do?"

"If you'll pick up my groceries, that would be great."

"I can do that," I said. I clapped my hands together. "He's going to be so surprised. I can't wait."

Though Grandma smiled, I sensed a sadness.

The following Saturday, we invaded Uncle Ted's home. His face lit up as he greeted us. Gunner and Mitch carried in extra chairs, while the rest of us brought in the food. Gifts were stacked on the coffee table. Grandma Janie started a pot of coffee, while Dad and Uncle Stan set up a folding card table.

Dad raised his brows. "We might need this later, Ted."

Uncle Ted laughed. "I could go for a round of poker. Who brought the beer?"

Gunner stepped forward. "Gotcha covered, Uncle. I brought Budweiser and BBQ."

"Well, you're all right." Ted told him.

Mitch seemed almost back to normal. Not overly talk-ative, but warm and cordial. At one point, I saw him gaze out the window to watch the Appaloosas next door.

I startled him from his thoughts. "Miss them?" I asked.

"Yeah, don't you?"

"I think about them a lot," I said. "But I'm sure you see them more than I do."

"I stop by when I can." He nodded towards our uncle, who was reclined and chatting with the crowd. "Look at his feet and ankles. They're so puffy."

Mitch was right. They were very swollen.

"It's a great turn-out," I said. "The party was Grandma's idea."

"Go figure."

About then, Aunt Katie made an announcement. "Food's ready. Come and get it!"

We lined up, paper plates in hand, and closed in on the BBQ ribs, roasted chickens, and casseroles. There was a large pot of green beans with ham, and another with homemade chili.

My Momma made a request. "Eat up, but be sure to save room for birthday cake."

Uncle Ted's ears perked up. "What kind did you make for me?"

Aunt Katie smiled and wrapped an arm around his shoulders. "Now Uncle Ted, don't we always make your favorite?"

He broke out in a huge grin. "German chocolate? I cer-tainly hope you brought more than one?"

Momma winked at him. "We brought one for the guests and another just for you."

After cake, candles and a birthday song, a poker game was underway. I helped Mom and my aunt clean the kitchen. Then we took our coffee and joined Grandma in the living room, where we caught up on neighborhood events. Every now and then, we stopped our conversation to laugh at the card game chatter. As usual, Gunner was winning big, which got him a good share of ribbing from the others.

Mitch became jittery as the evening drew on. Finally, he threw down his hand and gave Gunner a dirty look. "I'm out."

Gunner gathered the cards and began to shuffle. He looked up once to return my stare.

Uncle Stan stood and pulled on his coat. "I need to smoke; dare I brave the cold."

Grandma attempted to console him. "My almanac says another month of this, then we should expect an early spring."

Uncle Stan nodded his head. "That works for me, Janie. I'm ready for fishin' weather. If I get the freezer stocked up, we'll be all set for a July fourth fish fry." He laughed at himself, "Try saying that fast."

"At the crossing?" I suggested.

Uncle Stan gave me a thumbs up, then he and Dad walked onto the porch. Mitch left the table to pour himself a cup of coffee.

"Blackbirds," Uncle Ted mumbled.

Gunner looked up from flipping through the cards. "What did you say?"

Uncle Ted explained. "Oh, I was thinking about something that happened to me a long time ago. I guess I was around your age. I'd been fishing at the river all day. It was getting hot, so I gathered up my stuff to leave.

I was almost to the crossing when I noticed two men standing in the distance. It wouldn't have seemed odd, lots of folks came there to fish, but these two were dressed in black from head to toe. And they appeared to be in a confrontation, though I never heard a single word."

Mitch sipped his coffee and followed Ted's story.

Uncle Ted laughed and shook his head, as if making fun of himself. "As I got closer to my truck, the heat was rising from the rocks, like little waves. I kept a watch on the men, and judging by their body language, I thought I might have to break them up. I was about two hundred yards out, and then I stopped to set down my things. When I looked up, they had turned."

By now, we were all sucked in.

"Turned? How do you mean?" Gunner asked.

Uncle Ted answered without humor. "Into blackbirds."

Mitch howled. "Come on now, you left out the part about the moonshine in your ice chest, right?"

But Uncle Ted was dead serious. "No, nephew, I didn't."

Grandma's voice came forth, strong and clear. "Shapeshifters? I've heard tales about them. Legends say they can change from human to animal, then back again."

"Could have been an omen," Gunner said.

Aunt Katie rubbed her arms, "Oh, I just got goose-bumps. So, what happened next?"

Uncle Ted shrugged. "The birds just pecked around in the dirt. I walked closer, expecting them to fly away, but they didn't. It really shook me up." He pointed at Mitch. "And after that, I went home and got drunk. I've probably been back there a hundred times since, and haven't seen anything unusual."

My Dad and Uncle Stan walked back through the door. After a quick look around the room, they stopped in their tracks. Uncle Stan blurted out, "What the hell did we miss?"

Mitch pulled on his denim jacket. "A bunch of non-sense."

"Why don't you stay a spell?" Uncle Ted said. "What's wrong? Ants in your pants?"

Gunner peered at Mitch suspiciously.

Mitch laughed. "Yeah, I guess you could say that." He shook Ted's hand and said goodnight.

My uncle blinked back tears and spoke in Cherokee, "Gvgeyui."

"I love you, too, Uncle."

After Mitch closed the door, Aunt Katie spoke up. "Was he upset about something?"

Everyone looked to Grandma Janie.

She scooted forward and placed her coffee cup on the table. "Maybe, but mostly at himself. He has an addiction, and it's to the point where something must be done. I live with regret over my Julia's death, and I'll always wonder what else I could have done for her. But I won't allow this to happen to my family again."

"I share your guilt, U-lv," Uncle Ted addressed her in Cherokee as "sister."

The room became serious and silent, except for Gunner shuffling the cards. He continued to rearrange the deck over and over.

My Momma raised her hands, in question. "So, what do you suggest? A family meeting or something? We reasoned with Julia until we were blue in the face, but it didn't faze her at all."

"What can we do, other than insist he commit himself to a hospital?" Katie asked.

"I'm not sure I agree with locking him away," Ted said, "but he definitely needs treatment, and not medications like Julia was on."

The room buzzed with chatter. I continued to watch Gunner. Finally, he tossed the deck of cards to the middle of the table and stood. "Just a fair warning, Mitch probably won't listen. Take my word for it. But I'm with you, whatever you decide to do."

Three days later, our family members gathered on Mitch's front porch. Gunner stood at the very back. Uncle Ted knocked on the door and called out. When Mitch moved the curtain to look outside, his face froze in horror. He jerked the door open. "Shit, what happened?"

Ted placed a hand on Mitch's shoulder. "Everything's fine, we'd just like to run some things by you. May we come in?"

Mitch turned his confused expression to Grandma. "What's going on here?"

We seated ourselves in the living room, where his coffee table was strewn with liquor bottles and assorted paraphernalia. Grandma Janie began. "Mitch, I'm not going to beat around the bush. We're here because we know what you're involved in. We care about your health, as well as your future, so please listen. I believe it's time that you consult an addiction specialist for some help. There are a number of facilities in Tahlequah that provide these services. I won't stand back and watch drugs take your life away, as they did your mother's. We're all here for you, day or night, and we want to help with your recovery."

Though obviously humiliated, Mitch listened to us, and wiped the occasional tear. With my turn coming up, I could feel my stomach roll. I decided to keep my words short, after having said my piece at the river crossing. I reminded him that he had my love and support.

Gunner was last to speak. His comments were honest, but stern. "You and I have gone over this before, and I feel like I've tried everything already: I've cursed at you. I've swept this ugly shit under the rug. I've tried to reason with you, to no avail. Like Grandma said, we're all genuinely concerned for you. You should take advantage of our support, and make an effort to get well. We don't expect it to happen overnight, and we don't expect it to be easy. If you need us, just reach out. We'll go with you to therapy, or whatever it takes. All we ask is that you take your treatment seriously."

Mitch glared at Gunner as if he had been double-crossed. Uncle Ted sensed the tension between his great-nephews, and gave Mitch a reassuring pat on the back. "You can do this; I know you can."

Later, I pulled Gunner in for a hug, and whispered, "I can't tell you how much you amaze me." He smiled. "Let's just hope Mitch is hearing us."

Mitch had very little to say, but admitted to his weaknesses, and promised to deal with them. "I wish I had a good excuse for myself, but unfortunately, I don't. I should have known better. You supported my mom through thick and thin, you helped raise me, and now I've disappointed you."

"Grandson, I realize you haven't had it easy. You're only human. Don't get help just to please us. We can't save your life…Only you can do that."

Though Gunner hoped Mitch would resign from The Foxhole, he agreed to cut down his hours instead. Mitch entered a group therapy program, and committed to two sessions per week.

A few weeks passed before we began to see glimpses of Mitch's former, beautiful self. He made time for Grandma Janie, and on one of their visits, she taught him how to make homemade biscuits. He dedicated Saturdays to Uncle Ted. The two of them frequented their old fishing holes, and kept the ice chest alcohol-free. Mitch's relationship with Gunner became less strained, and it was great to see them joking together again. The rest of us supported his progress with encouragement and prayers.

You're never ready to lose a loved one, regardless of how much time you had to prepare. When Uncle Ted didn't make his morning walk to see the Appaloosas, his neighbor, Molly, became worried. She knocked on his door, but there was no answer. She quickly called Mitch, who raced right over. Our uncle had passed from this life peacefully, in his own bed, deep in the night.

When I received the news from my mom, I left work immediately. By the time I arrived at Uncle Ted's place, there were several cars in the driveway. Mitch and Gunner were on the porch. I hugged them, then went inside. Grandma was sad, but attempting to be strong. Mom and Aunt Katie had already phoned Ted's children, Kathryn and Paul.

A couple of hours later, a call came from Kathryn, saying that she and Paul had decided on a simple graveside service. I walked back to the porch to tell Gunner and Mitch. We sat quietly for a while. Gunner flipped the blade of his pocket knife in and out. Mitch seemed a million miles away, falling apart on the inside, no doubt.

Gunner spoke up. "One of us should call Lucas. He needs to know."

"I'll do it," I said. I went to the phone and dialed information. Once I had the construction company's phone number, I called, and the receptionist promised to locate Lucas and have him call me.

I returned to the porch, and the longer I sat, the more I stewed. I had to get it off my chest. "A simple graveside service?" I shook my head. "Seems like our Texas cousins just want to get Uncle Ted buried and forgotten. Like his death is an inconvenience to their busy schedules."

Gunner gave me a sharp look. "That's a little harsh, Sara."

Mitch stood. "It's the truth, Gunner. They rarely even called him, so why would they give a shit about his service? We should be planning the funeral ourselves."

Gunner leaned back in his chair, the voice of reason. "I understand, but it's not our place."

"So, what if they've made the arrangements? We could still do something special for Uncle Ted," I said.

Mitch nodded. "What are you thinking?"

I sighed. "I'm not sure, but something he would like."

Mitch jumped off the porch and headed for the gate. "I have an idea. I'll be in touch later."

Gunner watched him drive away. "I hope this doesn't push Mitch over the edge. He's been doing so well lately."

Aunt Katie came to the door. "Sara, Lucas is holding on the line."

Four days later, I rode with my parents to the hillside cemetery. We parked and walked to our family plot. The day was clear, and we could see for miles around. Mitch arrived ahead of us, just as we had secretly planned—and he wasn't alone. Spirit, Lady, and Aspen were with him, bathed and groomed. Gunner, Mitch, and I had also arranged for a Cherokee flutist to be there. Much of our community gathered to pay their respects.

The service was about to begin, when Lucas arrived and rushed to my side. He'd driven through the night just to make it on time. His reverence for Uncle Ted touched my heart. The flutist, Edgar Wilson, played a beautiful rendition of the "Cherokee Morning Song." Though laid to rest, our memories of Theodore Red Eagle, would live on infinitely.

We gathered at Ted's home after the funeral. Neighbors and friends brought in food and served us dinner. Grandma held up exceptionally well all day, but even so, I didn't want her to be alone that night.

After Lucas drove us to her home, she hugged us, then turned in early. I switched off the lights, except for a small lamp in the corner of the living room. Lucas and I settled on the sofa for a movie. It was a little awkward at first, and we kept the conversation casual. The movie was dull and boring, so we turned our attention to one another. As the night wore on, we became more comfortable. Before we even knew it, we were sitting closer together.

"Ted's service turned out nice," Lucas said.

I agreed. "Yes, it did. I don't know what we're going to do without him."

He took my hand in his. "I'll never forget all the good times."

"I'll miss his funny stories. Holidays will never be the same," I said.

He squeezed my hand gently.

I leaned closer. "I'm glad you're here, Lucas."

"This is where I should be," he said.

I put my head on his shoulder.

"Let me know if you're tired and I'll head on home," he whispered.

"No," I said. "I'm fine, but what about you? You must be exhausted after the long drive?"

He kissed my forehead. "I'm good, but don't tell Mitch and Gunner. They tried to get me out to the bar tonight."

I intertwined my fingers with his. "Out of curiosity, does Gunner know about us?"

"Mitch must have told him," Lucas said. "Gunner gave me a good-natured warning after the service."

"Oh, a warning about what?" I asked.

"He said I better treat you right or I'll be dealing with him and Mitch. I'm not scared, though."

He nudged me playfully.

Around one a.m., I walked him to the porch. When I stopped on the steps, he turned to face me. He was standing on the ground, and we were eye to eye. A breeze blew strands of hair across my face. He brushed my long waves aside and kissed me on the forehead. "Dinner tomorrow night?" he asked.

I fought hard to contain my desires. I wanted to drown my sadness in his kisses, but we had agreed not to rush things. I ignored my yearning and gave him a sweet smile. "Sure, I'd love to."

After Lucas returned to Wyoming, his phone calls came nightly. I looked forward to the sound of his voice after a long day of work and study. He made me feel secure and needed. I checked off the days of my calendar in anticipation of his next visit. And despite my sorrow for the loss of Uncle Ted, life seemed pretty good.

I hadn't seen my cousins since the memorial service, but assumed no news was good news. I worried that Ted's death might hinder Mitch's recovery. A few days later, Gillie called and said she saw Mitch earlier, his truck was riddled with gunshot holes. My heart raced. "Are you positive," I asked?

"That's what it looked like," Gillie said. "You should check on him."

I hung up and called Mitch. No answer. I grabbed my keys and headed for The Foxhole.

The doors were locked, but there were a few vehicles out front, including Gunner's Trans Am. I banged on the front door and called his name. An unfamiliar man opened the door and stepped outside. He was tall, with a horseshoe mustache and piercing blue eyes. "Can I help you, hun'?"

I cringed and wondered why people I don't even know call me, "Hun'?"

"Yeah," I said. "I'm looking for my cousin, Gunner. Is he busy?"

The man took his hand from the pocket of his leather jacket. "Well forgive my manners. I'm Lance. Gunner and I go way back."

My eyes widened as I shook his hand. So, this was Lance. Gunner stepped outside. "What's up, Sara?"

Lance interrupted. "Sara? He mentioned you when we were back in 'Nam. Don't mind me; if you two need to talk, our meeting can wait."

I studied Gunner's expression, which told me he was stressed and this wasn't the best time. So, instead of asking about Mitch, I drummed up a lame excuse for my visit. "Umm, it's really no big deal. Grandma needs some yard work done. Just call me later."

Gunner nodded. "Of course. I'll be in touch."

Gunner turned and went inside. He didn't even say goodbye. Alone again with Lance, I caught his lingering gaze. He sort of creeped me out, but I wasn't sure why.

"It was nice to meet you, Sara. Come by later and I'll buy you a beer."

I walked away and whispered under my breath. "Fat chance."

My next stop was Mitch's house. But of course, he wasn't there. I left a note on the door, asking him to call me. That night, I tossed and turned in bed. Who could have shot at Mitch's pickup? And why was Lance hanging around our town? I had a bad feeling deep in my gut, and I couldn't stop worrying. I sat up in bed. Why hadn't Mitch called? Damn him.

A couple of days passed, and still no word from Mitch. So, I called Gillie, and asked what she had heard. "Paulette's here right now. You should come on over."

After I arrived at Gillie's house, Paulette told me the word on the street, which was that Mitch had a falling out with Chester Owens again. It started as an argument in the bar's parking lot, but without Gunner there to step in, things turned physical.

Mitch punched Chester, and knocked him to the ground. As Mitch drove away, Chester retrieved a shotgun from his own pickup and fired. "I wonder if this is what brought Lance to town?" I asked. Paulette shrugged. Then I asked her what I really didn't want to know.

"Do you believe Mitch is using again?"

She hesitated. "I'm not sure if he's using again, Sara. But there's something else, and I hate to be the one to tell you."

My heart skipped a beat.

"The problems between Gunner and Mitch weren't just over his using meth. He's also been *selling* it."

I stood there in shock. "Are you positive? Why haven't I heard about this?"

"Because Gunner protected you from it. Don't blame him, though. He only has so much control over The Foxhole. Chester runs that show."

"What about Lance?"

"I'm not sure, he's pretty mysterious. But there's plenty of gossip flying around. People are connecting the bar to a drug operation. I really hate it for Gunner's sake. We all know this isn't what he signed up for."

I returned home; heartsick and worried. The phone rang, and it was Grandma Janie. A winter storm was moving our way, with possible tornadic activity ahead of it. I packed an overnight bag and drove to her house. It was February 22, 1977. We watched the weatherman confirm the winter storm warning on tv.

She sighed. "Hopefully the bad stuff will miss us. Keep the tv on so we can hear the alerts. I'm going to try to rest before it hits. Goodnight."

After Grandma hugged me and went to bed, I wrapped myself in a blanket and pulled the phone cord to the porch. I called Lucas and told him what I learned from Paulette earlier.

He listened until I finished. "Sara, you can't fix anything. That's Mitch's place. Promise me you'll leave it alone?"

"But I just want to see Mitch, and make sure he's okay. I realize that I can't actually help him."

Lucas stood his ground. "I have a bad feeling, Sara, and my feelings don't lie. I don't want to see you involved in Mitch and Gunner's affairs. Do I have your word?"

I struggled, but the last thing I wanted to do was disappoint him. "Okay. I'll back off."

He pressed harder. "But do I have your word?"

I tried to speak, but the words failed me at first.

"Baby," he whispered.

I knew in my gut that Lucas was right. "You have my word," I promised. "I'll stay away."

We said goodnight and hung up, but I wasn't sleepy. I remained there in the dark until sleet pelted the roof. The wind began to stir, so I walked to the edge of the porch to inspect the sky. Storm clouds were moving in. A barren tree swayed in the moonless night. A warbling sound filled the air. I scanned the yard, and saw nothing unusual. A chill ran down my spine.

I was about to go inside when the sound came again. Louder this time. As lightning flashed, I saw an owl in a tree close to the porch. It ruffled its feathers, looked at me with its large eyes and called out again. I remembered the old tales. And Lucas said he had a bad feeling. I didn't know what to do. I thought about waking Grandma, but decided not to worry her yet.

I checked my watch; it was two a.m., closing time at the bar. I stepped inside the front door and picked up the phone. I hesitated and hung up. I made a few steps toward my bedroom, but turned and went back to the phone. My body shivered as I dialed The Foxhole. It rang several times before I gave up. Despite my promise to Lucas, I wanted to see if my cousins were safe, that's all. What could it hurt?

I grabbed my purse, and ran out the door and across the porch. When my foot hit the icy step, I lost my balance and tumbled to the ground. I pulled myself to my knees, then inspected my scraped and bloody palms. Lightning lit up the entire sky, and I saw the owl take flight. It was gone. Hopefully, a good sign. Shame overcame me. I had no business going out in this storm, and just because of an owl? How silly. I'd stay here and honor my promise to Lucas. I stood and went back inside.

"Sara, wake up." Grandma touched my arm. "The roads are icy. You'll need extra time to get to work."

I jumped out of bed and hurried to get ready. When I came into the kitchen, I heard the front door slam.

Grandma looked up from her bowl of oatmeal. "Who could that be?"

My Mom came rushing into the kitchen without a stitch of makeup on, her face wet with tears. The image of the owl flashed into my mind, and a sick feeling clenched my gut.

Grandma asked, "What happened, Anna?"

Momma shook her head. "Stan called. He asked that we come right away. That's all I know."

Grandma and I grabbed our coats and followed Momma out the door. My nerves were in knots. The short drive to my aunt and uncle's home seemed to take forever. There was a sheriff's vehicle parked out front. We rushed inside and found Katie and Stan huddled together on the sofa. Two officers were leaving. They nodded politely as we passed them. We stood in the middle of the room, in fear of the news.

Aunt Katie reached out for Grandma. "Oh Momma, my boy, he's gone! Gunner is gone!"

My Grandmother gasped, then shook her head back and forth. "No. Please, no..."

My Mom fell to her knees and sobbed like I'd never seen before. Grandma went to Katie and pulled her close. Uncle Stan covered his face with his hands. I wasn't sure what to do, except to go to Mom's side. When I took her hand, I could feel her heart crumble into a million pieces.

Several minutes passed with no words spoken. Grandma pointed to the phone. "Sara, call Mitch and tell him to get over here."

Uncle Stan spoke. "He can't come. They took him to the E.R. to get checked out. I tried to see him when…" he swallowed hard. "When I identified Gunner. The officers wouldn't let me in." He stood abruptly and paced the floor.

Grandma and I looked at each other. This had to be a mistake. Gunner couldn't be gone. My Dad hurried through the doorway. His face drained of color when he saw Momma on her knees. The two of us lifted her to her feet, then she collapsed in his arms. I had to turn away. I moved to the nearest window to cry in private.

Aunt Katie wailed. "Oh James, they shot my Gunner. Who would do this to him? God, please help us!"

Grandma held Katie firmly in her arms, then looked to Uncle Stan. "Mitch was with Gunner when this happened?"

Uncle Stan nodded.

Grandma turned her attention back to me, voice cracking. "Honey, go call Lucas. He's like their brother."

I hurried down the hall to a bedside phone. After I explained to the construction company receptionist that we'd had another family emergency, she seemed shocked. "Oh my, I'll notify Lucas's foreman," she said. "I'm so sorry for your family."

When I returned to the living room, Mom was trying to coax Aunt Katie into taking a sip of coffee. Dad and I followed Uncle Stan outside. I swallowed the lump in my throat to ask, "Uncle Stan, did this happen at the bar?"

He lit a cigarette and hung his head. "No, it happened at the river crossing. I just can't wrap my head around it. Who would do this to Gunner?"

I felt a buzzing in my ears, and thought I might pass out. Dad sensed my panic and put a comforting hand on my shoulder. Moments later, Mom motioned me back inside.

"Lucas is holding for you," she said.

When I told Lucas, he sobbed miserably. Minutes went by before he spoke. It all started to sink in, and I just wanted to crawl in a corner and hide. Instead of begging Lucas to come home, I refrained. "You practically just left here, Lucas. Please don't feel as if you have to come home."

"But I need to be there," he said, "or I'll never forgive myself."

"No, don't beat yourself up. We understand."

I promised to call him later, then hung up the phone. As I sat in silence, my thoughts flew in a million directions. My nose burned like fire, as I wiped my tears. The thought of never seeing Gunner's face again was like a stab to my heart. How would my family possibly survive this?

Momma tapped on the door and came in. She sat down and held me, and rocked me gently back and forth. I gave way to my sobs. A few minutes later, she walked to the bathroom and brought back a cool, wet cloth. "Here, wipe your face and pull it together. I know it's hard, but we have to be brave for the others. Now go, Gillie and Paulette are waiting for you outside."

I walked out the front door. Dad was still sitting with Uncle Stan. Gillie and Paulette stood under a tree in the driveway. I walked to meet them, and Gillie hugged me first. Paulette puffed on a Virginia Slims cigarette. She took it from her mouth, then hugged me. "Sara, I heard Mitch was hurt, too. Why are they holding him at the sheriff's department?"

"I don't know anything," I said. "What else have you heard?"

She whispered, "Mack Hendrix found them on his way to work this morning. Mitch was lying beside Gunner's body. Mack said Mitch was out of his mind."

"I'm going to be sick!" I clutched my stomach. Gillie followed as I ran behind the tree. She dug in her purse for a tissue, and pushed it into my hand. "Maybe it's too soon to hear this, Sara. I'm so sorry."

I attempted to speak between heaves. "No, I need to know. What else?"

Paulette was hesitant to continue. "Mack mentioned their hands were bloody," she explained. "Like they'd had a fight, maybe?"

I turned to face her; my eyes wide with disbelief. "That can't be true."

Momma stepped onto the porch. "Sara, please take your grandma home. She said she needs to take her medicine and lie down for a bit."

As I turned to walk away, Gillie pulled me in for another hug. "I love you and I hope you get answers soon. Call me, okay?"

I wiped my mouth with the tissue. "I will."

Grandma gazed out the window in silence as we drove to her place. I helped her up the steps, then she walked to the corner of the porch. She scanned the field, as if looking for Gunner. I almost expected her to call out his name. But she dabbed her eyes with a handkerchief and turned to go inside.

That night, I was anxious to tell Lucas what I'd heard from Paulette. He said very little when I called, and I could feel his pain through the phone line. After we hung up, I put on my pajamas and sat on the bed. I stared into the darkness. It was the longest night of my life. My eyes were swollen and painful; I must have cried a thousand tears. The wind whipped and howled outside my window. I got up at three a.m. for a drink of water, and heard Grandma crying. She said something out loud. Maybe she was talking to Gunner? I placed a glass of water on her bedside table. "Call out if you need me," I told her.

The next morning, we went back to Aunt Katie's house. My Mom had spent the night there. She whispered as we came to the door, "Katie's finally resting. Stan left for a bit. Let's talk out here for a few minutes."

We sat down and Mom reached for Grandma's hands. "Mother, I know this will be hard on you, but you must know that Mitch isn't being cooperative with the detectives. He refuses to give them any details about Gunner's murder. Sheriff Calhoun might be forced to file charges on him. Stan is at the sheriff's department now, trying to see Mitch."

Grandma was stoic. "Mitch didn't hurt Gunner. I can promise you that."

Mom sighed. "I know, but what we can do?"

The days between Gunner's death and his funeral were a blur. Grandma Janie didn't have the strength to attend the service. Miss Ada—Lucas's granny and a longtime friend—stayed to look after her.

At the church, Aunt Katie barely looked up; but kept her face buried in Uncle Stan's suit sleeve. Some of Gunner's schoolmates served as pallbearers. Another played "The Old Rugged Cross" on a fiddle.

Brother Jasper conducted Gunner's eulogy, which mentioned his childhood days, his bravery while serving our country, and his love of family and community. At the cemetery, the pain of Uncle Ted's death was still fresh. He'd always been a pillar of strength for the family, but I'm sure even he would've struggled with this tragedy.

At the end of the service, Brother Jasper led us in prayer. He paused occasionally to dab his tears with a handkerchief. I studied Uncle Stan and the dark circles under his eyes. God love him; as he struggled so hard to hold up for Aunt Katie.

That night, I sat in front of Grandma's television, but didn't hear a single word. I was numb. As I awaited Lucas's call, I wondered how our family had even survived this difficult, heart-wrenching day. Grandma told us long ago that there would be days that only the Grace of God would carry us through. She wasn't eating much. I cried to Lucas on the phone, "Considering how sad and weak she is, I've decided to live with her for a couple of months."

On the morning of Mitch's arraignment hearing, Grandma insisted I pick her up, though Momma and Aunt Katie had discouraged her from attending. They seated Mitch before we were allowed inside the courtroom. The hearing took thirty minutes. Mitch never even glanced our way. His face was swollen and bruised.

We learned very little on that day, most of which had been reported in the newspaper. A log truck driver had discovered Mitch Kincaid and Gunner Lane on his way to work. Mitch was beaten and in shock. Gunner was deceased, a gunshot wound to his chest. There was a handgun on the scene. The evidence showed that a fight between the two of them had presumably turned deadly.

The judge told Mitch he was prepared to file a charge of first-degree manslaughter, punishable by up to fifteen years in prison. When he asked Mitch how he wanted to plead, Mitch refused to answer. The judge told Mitch he had the right to a public defender, and set another hearing for two weeks out. The courtroom was then adjourned. Grandma called Mitch's name as he was being led away, but he didn't turn around.

I helped Grandma into my Jeep, and she asked me to drive to the cemetery.

"Are you sure?" I asked.

She nodded.

When we got there, I took her arm and guided her to the family plot. She studied the flowers on Gunner's grave, and repositioned them to her liking. She kneeled to pat the earth, as if tucking him in.

I stood back and gave her some privacy while she prayed. I fumed silently over the day's events. What was Mitch thinking? Didn't we deserve an explanation? I wanted to scream at the top of my lungs.

Afterward, we drove to the farm to find Lucas sleeping on the porch swing, cowboy hat covering his face. He jumped up and ran to my Jeep, opened Grandma's door and assisted her out. They cried together as he hugged her. "It's okay," he said. "I've got you."

He wrapped an arm around her shoulders and walked her to the house. "I hear you haven't had much of an appetite," he said. "If I cook supper, will you try to eat?"

She shrugged. "You shouldn't go to all that trouble over me."

"My parents sent some backstrap. I'll season it, wrap it up in bacon and throw it in the oven. How about mashed potatoes and gravy, too?"

"It's been a while since I've had venison," Grandma said.

"So, do we have a deal?"

Grandma Janie grinned. "I'll make the biscuits." It was the first time she'd smiled in days.

After our meal, I walked Lucas to his truck. His eyes were puffy and bloodshot, and I could tell he was exhausted from his long drive from Wyoming.

"As much as the rest of us have begged her to eat," I said, "you just waltzed in here and fed her. And she even had seconds."

Lucas pulled me in for a hug. "I have a way with women and horses." He kissed me on the cheek. "I still can't believe all this. It's just so messed up."

Standing there in the comfort of his arms, I wished for time to stand still.

The next day, Lucas went to see Mitch at the county jail, only to be told that Mitch had refused all visitations. That night, Lucas treated me to dinner and a movie, which helped take our minds off things for a while. He was only in town for three days, so we made the best of our time together. I tried to prepare myself for his goodbye, but I cried like a baby when he left, and for hours after.

On the day of Mitch's sentencing, our family gathered in the courtroom. We watched as he was led in. He glanced our way this time, but only for an instant. His expression was unreadable. My whole body trembled as he stood with the public defender, Travis Goodwin. When the judge asked Mitch for his plea, Mitch looked him straight in the eye. "I plead guilty, Your Honor."

The courtroom was aghast, and Mitch's lawyer seemed just as shocked as the rest of us. His face turned bright red, and he asked permission to approach the bench. I could hear bits and pieces of his conversation with the judge. "I don't know what he's thinking," Travis said. "His prints weren't on the weapon, Your Honor!"

The room buzzed. The judge shifted in his chair and pounded the gavel. Mitch turned to face us and right then and there, we witnessed his silent admission. He locked eyes with Grandma, and studied her face like it would be the very last time.

Weeks later, Mitch received a fifteen-year sentence for manslaughter. The prosecution had grounds to claim that during their altercation, Gunner pulled a handgun in self-defense. He didn't shoot, but hit Mitch on the head with it. Mitch overpowered Gunner and, one way or another, the gun went off, killing Gunner.

All we knew was the same story as the one the newspapers reported. Mitch refused all contact with the outside world. Then one scorching, midsummer's day, he was bused to a prison a hundred miles away.

I had the strangest dream that night. I was driving down a dirt road on a beautiful sunny day. The road seemed long, as I sang with the radio. But then the sky turned dark, and the miles rolled on and on. It seemed like I'd never get to where I was going. I drove faster, looking for an exit.

A light appeared in the distance, so I sped up. But just as I drew near it, a large owl with red eyes flew directly into my windshield. I woke up in a cold sweat, my heart pounded in my chest. I tried to go back to sleep, but kept thinking about the dream. I realized that for the first time ever, my cousins were completely out of my life.

I tried to write letters to Mitch, but they always turned angry. I was desperate for answers. Why wouldn't he talk to us? Did we deserve this silence from him? I wanted to lash out and call him terrible names. The writing always ended with me tearing up the letters and throwing them away.

Mom, Grandma and Aunt Katie dealt with grief in their usual way; that summer, our garden was more bountiful than ever before. We shared the surplus with neighbors, our church family, and the Waya senior citizens center. One Saturday, after a long, hot day of canning, we carried our iced teas to the front porch.

"Sara, how's college going?" Aunt Katie asked. She wiped her brow with the back of a hand.

"Busy, but well," I said. "I meet myself coming and going at times."

She smiled. "Well, your Uncle Stan and I are so proud of you. All of your dedication and hard work will definitely pay off. Just hang in there, baby."

"Thanks, Aunt Katie. I look forward to graduating in December."

Mom and Grandma rocked slowly on the porch swing. "Then what?" Aunt Katie asked.

I went on to explain how much I enjoyed working with Carl, and how she had become my mentor.

Grandma Janie nodded. "Carl is an intelligent woman with a good soul."

I agreed. "Yes, and I'm so inspired by her, that I hope to become a pharmacist one day."

Grandma Janie patted my hand. "*Osda!* Bless you, Granddaughter. That's wonderful. I'm glad you inherited my interest in medicine. My teachings will definitely come in handy."

Aunt Katie grinned. "A pharmacist in our family? That's lovely. And, what about Lucas?"

My face lit up at the mention of his name. "He's planning to move back soon," I said. "Hopefully by the end of this year."

Aunt Katie shot a suspicious glance at Mom and Grandma, then pressed for more. "Anything else you might share? I love good news."

My cheeks began to tingle. "Um, not really. I mean, not yet. We've decided to take things slow."

My Mom jumped in. "Which is a good thing. Your studies need to take priority."

Aunt Katie laughed and slapped her thigh. "Anna Belle, come on. Don't tell me you and James aren't looking forward to grandchildren? Just imagine how beautiful they'll be."

Momma held up a forefinger. "You're getting ahead of us, sister."

"Actually, I've imagined…" I noted their surprised expressions. "But not anytime soon."

Aunt Katie winked mischievously.

Grandma gazed across the field, longingly. "I can't wait to see children playing here again."

On a cloudless day in June, I stood at the side of Gillian Renae Ferrell as she became Mrs. Jason "Jay Bob" Matthews. In a very simple ceremony, they exchanged vows in the Methodist church, which his family had been attending for decades. After a short reception, the happy couple left for their honeymoon on the Gulf Coast. Jay Bob had recently completed welding school and accepted a job in Tulsa, which is where they planned to make their home. I was already looking forward to weekend getaways at their place.

That night, Lucas and I snuggled on Grandma's porch swing, with crickets chirping all around us. I lifted my head from his shoulder. "Wasn't the wedding beautiful?"

"Yeah, it was. I like that kind of wedding."

"What do you mean?"

"Short and sweet. Casual. Unpretentious."

I nodded. "Less is more, or so I've heard."

He shrugged. "Maybe I'm just a simple kind of guy?"

I winked at him. "Nothing wrong with that."

His expression turned serious. "By the way, how do you think things are going so far? Between us, I mean?"

"Things are great. I have no complaints, other than you living so far away."

His lips brushed my cheek. "I'm glad to hear you say that, especially after the call I received from Bar S Construction."

I became giddy with excitement. "Bar S Construction? I didn't know you applied."

He nodded. "I did. And they made me an offer. You're lookin' at their new foreman. I'll start on the first of next month."

I pulled him closer. "*Yeesss!* I'm so happy."

He laughed. "And I'm so happy you're happy. But I still have to go back to Wyoming to give notice and pack up. When I get back here, I'll have a whole week off before I start my new job."

I gave him a flirty look. "Have you made any plans?"

Lucas grinned. "Oh, I might sleep in. And take my dad fishing." He paused, as if deep in thought.

I scooted closer. "Yeah, what else?"

"I'll ride my horse."

I caressed his thigh. "And?"

He pulled me onto his lap. "And make out with you, if that's okay?"

I didn't answer, but pressed myself into him, kissing him with all the passion I had. A few minutes later, he reluctantly pulled back. "My Lord, girl! You better simmer down, or else we'll have to sneak off to the cellar."

The next evening, I prepared for a date with Lucas. While soaking in a rose-scented bubble bath, my butterflies stirred with anticipation. I dried off and pulled a paisley print dress from its hanger. Then I slipped my feet into a pair of strappy sandals. My butterflies were soaring high by the time Lucas's truck turned down Blackberry Lane. I hurried out to greet him. We hugged Grandma goodbye, and drove into the night. After crossing the cattle guard, he shifted his truck into park, pulled me close and kissed me until my head spun.

I giggled. "What was that all about?"

"You've been on my mind all day long."

He shifted into drive and we were rolling again.

On the way, we decided on a place for dinner; the nicest steakhouse in Tahlequah. But despite the candlelit atmosphere and delicious food, I wasn't hungry at all.

"What's wrong?" he asked.

I put my fork and knife down. "Nothing, I'm fine."

He gazed across the table. "You look really beautiful tonight."

"Thank you."

"Why are you being so bashful?" Lucas asked.

I shrugged.

He pushed his plate aside, his eyes searched mine. "Do you want to leave?"

"Yes," I said.

He opened his wallet and threw cash on the table. "All right, let's go."

We sat in his truck as a light rain beaded the windshield. He reached to caress my arm. "What would you like to do? Wanna' go dancing?"

"Not really," I whispered. I didn't know how to tell him. But before I could, he cut to the chase.

"You know what? You've been on my mind for months, and now we're finally alone together. Please don't think I'm a creep, but all I want to do is take you to the nearest hotel. I don't care if it's cheap, or on the seedy side of town, as long as it's close."

I buckled up. "Let's go."

His eyes went wide. "You're serious?"

I didn't answer, but smiled from ear-to-ear.

He fumbled with his keys and the truck raced from the parking lot. He stopped at a hotel just down the street, and walked around to open my door. When I turned to jump out, he pulled my legs to the edge of the seat, then leaned into me. "I'll go pay. Don't go anywhere."

It seemed like he was gone for hours. I was nervous and urged my wild butterflies to settle down. Fifteen minutes later, Lucas hurried back and took me by the hand. He unlocked the door to our dimly lit room. I stepped inside and stood still for a moment. He wrapped his arms around me from behind, pushed my hair aside, and kissed my neck. Despite my eagerness, I pointed to the bathroom. "Be right back."

In the bathroom, I took off everything except my pink lace underwear. Until now, my few sexual experiences had taken place in a vehicle, so I wanted tonight to be unforgettable. I fished through my purse for a bottle of perfume, and spritzed the soft scent across my stomach. Then I checked my reflection in the mirror, tousled my hair a bit, and slipped out the door.

Lucas stood facing the window, shirtless. His hair reached the middle of his back. I moved close and caressed its softness. He turned and leaned down for a kiss. Then his hands scooped me up and lifted me to his waist. I wrapped my legs around his body and clutched his shoulders. His muscles felt like sculptured steel. He lowered me onto the bed and whispered, "I'm crazy about you."

I traced his jawline with my finger. "Nobody's ever said that to me before." I slid my hands down his back and pulled his body closer. He unsnapped his jeans and pushed them off, then kissed me harder and removed my bra. His tongue traced my neck, before inching down to my breasts. I needed him now, all of him.

After he pulled away my panties, he didn't rush. Instead, he took the time to make sure I was totally at ease. He made love to me, gently at first, then with a steady intensity that gave me a pleasure I had never known. Our passion soared, peaked, and gently subsided. We clung to one another, still panting. He kissed me slowly, again and again, until my body released the grief it had been holding inside. Tears spilled down my face. We breathed each other in, laughed together, and explored one another for hours.

Afterward, we drove the rain-drenched streets to the farm. I noticed Lucas's face in the dashboard light; his soft, contented smile. A warm and blissful feeling came over me. Could this be love?

A few weeks later, Lucas moved back to Waya. He planned to live with his parents temporarily. I suggested that he call cousin Paul to ask about renting my uncle's house. Paul proposed a lease-to-buy option, and Lucas took him up on it.

Only days after Lucas arrived back to town, he wrote a letter to Mitch, asking to be placed on his visitation list. To my surprise, Mitch agreed to it.

Aunt Katie and Uncle Stan did their best to carry on without Gunner. They took short getaways, and sometimes asked my parents to go along. They visited places like Branson, Missouri, and New Orleans, Louisiana.

I continued to keep a close eye on Grandma Janie, and day by day, she was slowly getting back to herself again.

Despite the hurt from the absence of my cousins, things were coming together nicely for me and Lucas, and I was falling hard for him. I recall the day I helped him move into Uncle Ted's house. We drove by The Foxhole with a load of his belongings, and noticed that the parking lot was almost full of vehicles. Since Gunner's death, Pete, had taken over management. "Do you know what's strange to me?" I asked. "As close as they were, Lance didn't show up at Gunner's funeral. No flowers, no card, nothing."

Lucas nodded. "I agree with you. Very strange."

Since Uncle Ted's kids had already taken what items they wanted, his home was still furnished. As Lucas and I rearranged the furniture, we heard a knock at the door. I opened it to find Molly, the next-door neighbor, standing on the porch. I invited her in, and she informed us that one of the appaloosas—Aspen—had passed away a few days' prior. Since Aspen had not been sick, the veterinarian said she'd likely died of old age. Lucas and I looked at one another. After Molly left, I crumpled to the floor.

Lucas kneeled over me. "The horses are old, Sara. They've had really good lives."

"Don't you see? It's not just that, everything's changed so much." I cried.

Lucas pulled me close. "I know. But Ted was up in age before his health turned bad. We can't hold onto people forever."

"I've accepted that, but losing Gunner is like a bad dream that will never end." I explained.

A sudden bitterness crept into Lucas' voice. "In my opinion, Gunner should have listened to Grandma Janie. The Foxhole was a mistake from the start. I'd love to see that place burn to the damned ground."

"Do you believe there were others involved that night?" I asked.

"At the river crossing? Why do you say that?"

"Remember when I told you about Lance being in town?"

"Let's not make any assumptions." Lucas warned.

I searched his eyes. "What do you know?"

Lucas shook his head. "Nothing for certain. But I'm going to talk to Mitch, and until I do, please don't mention Lance's name in public, okay?"

I agreed. Grandma always said Lucas was wise beyond his years. My suspicions soon devoured me, and I had a new purpose; to uncover the truth about the night of Gunner's death, no matter how long it took.

Now that Lucas was on Mitch's visitation list, he began making monthly trips to the prison. It was important that he go, not only to keep Mitch's spirits up, but to gather details about the night of Gunner's death. Mitch avoided the subject, though, and was tight-lipped. My nerves were on edge every visitation day, as I waited anxiously for Lucas' return. But the report was always the same; Mitch looked either too-thin or depressed.

The mystery surrounding Gunner's murder remained in the back of our minds all the time. Though Grandma's deep sadness had subsided, she had little interest in leaving the farm, and chose to occupy herself at home and in the garden.

After Lucas' fourth visit to the prison, I rushed to his house, hopeful for news. He'd just walked in the door, still wearing his jacket and cowboy hat. I sat down at the kitchen table and waited for him to speak.

"He looks good." Lucas said. "He's been working out. He asked how everyone's doing. He told me he's reading his Bible and going to service on Sundays. That's great, isn't it?"

I took it all in, but failed to see anything substantial. "Yeah, I suppose," I said.

"Oh, he has a tattoo of Chief Joseph wearing a headdress. It covers most of his back. It's not bad for a prison tat."

I was unimpressed. "Honey, I know you don't want to rush Mitch, but did you even bring up Gunner's name?"

Lucas got a beer from the fridge. Stalling maybe? I pressed on. "I mean, is Grandma going to die before she has an explanation? This is torture…" I stood up. "And I'm so glad he's in church. How nice. Especially since he's put the rest of our family in hell."

"That's enough." Lucas said.

I lost control. "It's almost like he doesn't give a shit about our feelings. But, oh that's right, why should he? He's a murderer!"

Lucas slammed his beer into the sink. An explosion of suds spewed onto the kitchen floor. "You don't know that," he said. "And whether you wanna' hear it or not, there's a chance you'll never know, Sara. He pled guilty, and now he's serving his time. I understand why you want details. We all do. But has it ever occurred to you that he might be protecting us?"

"You're defending him? Seriously, just listen to yourself."

Lucas stood toe to toe with me. "No, you listen. I drive over 200 miles every month, not just for Mitch, but for your entire family. And after every damned trip, I get the same thing from you."

"The same thing?"

"When I get back here, you're up in my face practically asking for blood. Then I watch as your beautiful smile fades, and the hope drains from your body. Why are you attacking me? Am I just an easy target?"

I tasted my tears before I realized I was crying. Even worse, I didn't have an answer for him. "Since I'm making things so unpleasant for you," I said, "I'll just leave."

I snatched up my purse and bolted out the door. I jumped the steps and ran to the gate. But just as I reached for it, something stopped me in my tracks. What the hell was I thinking? Was I really going to allow Mitch's behavior to destroy my relationship with Lucas? This beautiful and selfless man loved me, after all.

I caught my breath and turned around. I hurried back inside and into the kitchen. Lucas leaned against the fridge with his arms crossed. I wiped my tears away and prepared for the worst. "You don't have to go to that prison on my account," I said. "I wouldn't blame you for never going back."

"I want to go." he said. "He's my brother."

I stepped closer. "I'm so ashamed of my behavior. I could've said hello and given you a kiss before I starting asking all those questions. I'm sorry that I took you for granted."

He stood up straight. "I'm not the enemy, Sara. All I want is your love."

We fell into each other's arms and kissed desperately. Our frustration turned to passion. I pushed away his jacket and fumbled with the zipper of his pants. He backed me up against the kitchen table, slipped my sundress over my head and threw it across the room. Then he lifted me up and set me on the table.

"I love you, Lucas," I said. "I love you so much." We made love like never before; fierce, like a wildfire burning out of control. We were consumed with desire. Everything was suddenly different; the doubts gave way to complete trust.

Afterward, Lucas laid his head upon my heaving chest. "I love you, too. I always have."

Later, he grabbed a couple of apples and invited me for a walk. We strolled through the backyard, on past a trellis which was draped with dried vines, and to the fencerow. "Did you know Ted grew grapes?" Lucas asked.

I nodded. "He shared them with Grandma."

"I found a few bottles of homemade wine in the cellar." Lucas said.

"His kids left them behind?" I asked.

Lucas wrapped an arm around my shoulders. "That's alright, we'll save them for special occasions. It's what he would've wanted."

Spirit and Lady noticed us and came right over. We gave them pets as they enjoyed the apples.

I had to be sure that Lucas and I were on the same page. "I have no evidence, but I believe Mitch is innocent. It's my responsibility to help him, and I hope you'll support me?"

The corners of his mouth turned into a smile. "You know I'd go to the ends of the earth for you."

On New Year's Eve, I rushed to the farm after work, showered, then headed straight to Lucas' house. We planned to stay in, so I wore jeans, and a black turtleneck with a Sherpa vest. After I let myself in, I found Lucas on the back deck, standing over the grill. I strolled over and looked up at him affectionately. "*Mmm.* smells good, baby."

"I've been slaving over a hot stove all day." He pretended to wipe his brow. "But seriously, I hope you like everything."

I followed him to the kitchen and waited as he built my plate; filet mignon and baked potato, roasted carrots, and a colorful salad. "You're such a gentleman," I said. "I could really get used to this."

Lucas held up a bottle of Uncle Ted's wine. He poured, and I was taken by the rich crimson color. I lifted the glass and placed it under my nose. Then I closed my eyes and inhaled the scent of earth, fruit, and oak. I took the first taste, which felt silky on my tongue.

The experience wasn't as magical for Lucas, however. After a large gulp from his glass, he smacked his lips together. "Not bad at all." Then, he motioned to the oven. "There's a blackberry cobbler in there, not with just any old blackberries, mind you…Blackberry Lane blackberries."

I laughed. "Compliments of Grandma Janie's freezer, I'm guessing?"

"Yeah. I promised to save her a piece."

We dug into the delicious meal, and I was quite impressed. Afterwards, we had cobbler with vanilla ice cream. Then Lucas reached for his coat. "Wanna' go watch the sky? There's supposed to be a full Moon tonight. I'll make us a fire."

Who needed fireworks? I reached for a blanket and grabbed the bottle of wine. The night couldn't have been more perfect.

Lucas took some kindling and got the fire started. Soon, flames were dancing and flickering in front of us. We huddled together on an old bench, and passed the bottle back and forth.

"I thought about taking you dancing," Lucas said. "But since you worked all day, I liked this idea better." He pulled me closer. "Besides, I kinda' wanted you all to myself."

I giggled and kissed his cheek. My body felt a sudden rush of warmth. The wine was now in charge. We gazed up at the moon in all its glory.

"Have you ever seen anything so bright?" I asked. Lucas cocked his head to one side. "Come to think of it, yes." He slid onto his knees and pulled a small velvet box from his pocket. When he opened it, I gasped and covered my mouth with my hands. He tilted the box back and forth, allowing the emerald-cut diamond to reflect the light of the moon.

"Sara Elizabeth Ryan," he said, "if you'll marry me, I'll do my best to make all of your dreams come true."

My drunken butterflies stopped in mid-flight and waited for the answer.

"Yes, Lucas Matthew Crow, I'll marry you."

On the first of May--May Day--Gillie and Paulette arrived to Grandma's farm early. They carried a ladder to the big Oak and wrapped its lower limbs in white lights. Then they hung paper flowers from pastel ribbons, and draped tulle from its branches. It took half the day, and when they were finished, the tree was dressed beautifully for our wedding. The field of clover and yellow bitter weeds served as a perfect backdrop.

White tables were set with tapered candles and silver, all the elegance we needed. My bouquet was made of hydrangeas and jasmine, gathered by Grandma Janie from her own yard. She, Momma, and Aunt Katie helped me into my off-the-shoulder wedding gown. I stood before them and waited for their reactions.

Momma clasped her hands together. "You're just as beautiful as the first time I laid eyes on you."

Aunt Katie sniffled. "Oh Lord, I'm trying not to cry."

My Mom nodded. "Which is why my pocketbook is filled with tissues."

Grandma stepped close. "You're beautiful, Granddaughter. My heart is over-joyed." She handed me a small silver locket which was attached to a blue ribbon. "It belonged to your Aunt Julia."

I accepted it, and wrapped it around my wrist. "Thanks Grandma. I'm honored to wear it."

Gillie appeared with the final detail, and placed a home-made crown of flowers on my head. "I hope you like it."

I smiled. "It's beautiful."

They walked me to the porch, where I pulled up my hem and reached for Daddy's arm. We strolled across the grass, and to the tree, where he presented me to my groom: Lucas Crow--child dancer, protector, soulmate. Before friends and family, we pledged our loyalty through thick and thin, joy and sorrow. I gave him my heart like an offering of love; warm and of crimson, dangling from a chain of gold. We kissed.

Corks flew and laughter spilled as the sun began to set. Grandma looked beautiful in a pistachio-colored dress and a pair of pearl earrings that Gunner had given her a couple of years ago. My eyes searched the crowd for him and Mitch. My ears yearned for Uncle Ted's laughter. The wind whispered their names.

Lucas must have read my thoughts. "They're happy for us, you know."

Four

Homeward

I was officially Sara Elizabeth Crow, and settled happily into married life. I added a female touch to the house. Lucas' only request was, "Please don't go overboard with the pink."

Our days began early, and we didn't arrive home until dusk. Weekends consisted of chores and errands, as well as my studies. Despite our schedules, we made time for each other and our families. I'd grown increasingly close to Lucas's parents, Betty and Daniel, and to his Granny Ada. She loved to join us at the farm, where she and Grandma Janie would chat for hours.

Lucas and I were happy in Uncle Ted's house, and since the acreage was large enough to serve our future horse training business, we discussed the possibility of buying it. The well-built Antebellum-style home needed a few upgrades, which we looked forward to tackling. There were three bedrooms, so plenty of room for children, though I was in no hurry to get pregnant. Lucas, on the other hand, claimed to be ready at the drop of a hat. "Is there ever a perfect time for anything?" he questioned. "You just go with the flow and it all works out."

His philosophy didn't surprise me, as he handled stress very well. He was always the gentleman, patient and even-tempered. Lucas carried a quiet confidence that earned him great respect from his employer, as well as his con-struction crew. His parents had definitely raised him right.

On his next trip to visit Mitch in prison, he took our wedding pictures along. Mitch looked them over and asked questions, smiling from time to time--quite a change from his usual somber disposition. "Why is my grandmother sitting in most of these?" he asked.

Lucas explained that at nearly eighty years now, she found it hard to stand for long periods of time. It seemed to trigger something in Mitch, and he decided to spill his truths, right then and there.

"It was two a.m., and the parking lot had just cleared out," he told Lucas. "Gunner and Pete were cleaning up inside the bar. I watched the band pack up their van and drive off. An ice storm was moving in that night. I re-member sitting in my pickup outside, thinking how fast the temperature was dropping. That's when Chester walked up from behind.

"The weather was turning bad, with sleet on the ground. Gunner finally came outside. He glanced over, and made a motion with his head, telling me to follow his car. Chester rode with him. We ended up at the river crossing. It was very dark out there, so I flipped the cargo lamp on when I got out of my pickup. That's when I saw Lance standing on the bank.

"I assumed his helicopter was close, maybe just out of our sight, since that's usually how he traveled. He walked over to meet us. I figured I was about to be in the hot seat, so I was ready when Chester opened his fat mouth. It started out with just me and him going at it. He brought up all this shit he'd supposedly heard about me, then accused me of putting their entire operation in jeopardy. Of course, I denied it because I knew Chester had made it up. Lance and Gunner stayed out of it at first. Then Chester called me a lying' piece of shit, and that's when I shoved him. We were standing on slick rocks, and he slid and fell backward.

"Lance stepped in, with a look on his face I'll never forget. I stood there and took his threats, until he said, 'I oughta' kill your junkie ass.' I drew the line there. I was about to hit him, but Gunner grabbed my arm. You know how Gunner…was. He started reasoning with us, and told us to calm down, and he tried to get things under control. He pushed me aside and asked them what he could do to fix everything. Chester stepped up, and told Gunner they wouldn't even consider it. Then he laughed in Gunner's face.

"Lance yelled into a two-way radio, something like, 'Be ready.' The helicopter started up. Gunner's voice was desperate, still trying to work everything out. Lance told Gunner, 'It's too late. He's coming with me.' I wasn't sure what he meant by that, but Gunner knew. Something came over Gunner, and when he hit Lance, he dropped like a fly. But Lance got up, and then they really went at it. Gunner beat him down to the ground.

"Gunner was furious, and starting yelling at them, saying that he'd never agreed to any shady business at the bar. From the corner of my eye, I saw Chester run off, but I couldn't imagine where he was going. I was more concerned with Gunner's safety. While Lance was on the ground, he kicked Gunner's bad leg and knocked him down. Gunner rolled and was back on his feet right away. When Lance tried to get up, I saw my chance to take up the fight. I was ready to kill him. It was the only way. I lunged at him, but the next thing I knew, I was on my knees and I didn't know which way was up. I'd been hit from behind. Blood was dripping from my head onto the rocks.

"Lance yelled to Chester, 'Kill him!' That's when Gunner grabbed Lance by the throat and started to choke him. I heard Gunner say, 'You set me up. The bar was a sham from the start.' When I tried to stand, Chester's boots were in front of me. He kicked me in the gut, sending me backward.

"Chester knew I was down for a minute, so he rushed over to help Lance. He was holding a hand gun. I recognized it as Gunner's. Chester must have gotten it from Gunner's car. Gunner always had it on him at the bar, and carried it home every night. By then, I was halfway to my feet and yelled to warn Gunner. But he was like a wild animal with a grip around Lance's throat. Chester took aim. Gunner saw him and loosened his hands to let Lance fall.

"Gunner looked over his shoulder and shouted, 'Hand over my gun, Chester.' But Chester held his ground. He pointed it at Gunner's chest. Gunner threatened, 'Hand it over, you coward. You don't have the fucking balls to shoot me!'

"Chester looked to Lance, who was holding his throat and couldn't speak, but he shook his head real fast. It looked like he was trying to say, 'No.'

"I wasn't about to let Gunner take my bullet. Lance tried to yell but his voice was hoarse. 'Not him!'

"Gunner was closing in on Chester-- just a couple of steps away. I bolted for Chester, but the gun went off before I could reach him. I heard a scream, and at the time, had no idea it had come from me. I started seeing spots and fell. Next thing I knew, I was flat on my back. I wondered if it was all just a bad dream. As I laid there starring up at the trees, I remember seeing an owl fly over."

"Lance's voice was raging. He was going nuts on Chester. 'You shot the wrong man, you fucking moron!' I couldn't take my eyes off the sky because I didn't want to see anything else. Lance and Chester came and stood over me. Chester held the gun. I sat up and pressed my forehead to the barrel. 'Go ahead, do it,' I said. 'Kill me.'

"I begged them, over and over. Lance kneeled down in front of me. 'No, I have a better idea. Since you caused all this, you'll take responsibility for it. It makes perfect sense. Everybody in town knows that you and Gunner weren't getting along. You got in an argument, fought over the gun, and it went off. Just like that. And if I ever hear a different version coming from you, that sweet family of yours will start disappearing, one by one. We know who they are, and where they live.'

"They grabbed my arms and dragged me to Gunner's body. I knew I had nothing to lose, so I kicked Chester as hard as I could. Then I crawled to Gunner, and put my ear over his heart, but he was gone.

"I heard a strange voice come over Lance's radio. 'We have to go or this weather will shut us down.' That's when Chester rebounded and kicked me in the face. After I threw up, everything faded. I guess I passed out.

"We'd all be better off if I had frozen to death that night. It's only right that I pay for Gunner's death, and I'll be paying until the day I die. Gunner died defending me--a low-life, drug dealer."

Lucas cut in. "That wasn't the real you, Mitch. You were sick."

Mitch hung his head. "I should have been his keeper, not his killer. Now you know, but a risk comes with the truth, and I can't protect anyone from here."

Lucas recounted the entire story to me that night. "I finally have the truth," I said, "And no idea what to do with it." We let it soak in for a few days, then called our family together for a meeting at Grandma Janie's house. With everyone seated around the kitchen table, Lucas revealed the hard facts.

"Before we make any decisions," Lucas said, "keep in mind, there are dangerous men involved. Mitch took the rap for a reason, to protect you all. But whatever you decide to do, I'm with you one hundred percent."

Uncle Stan was furious. "Those sorry bastards are walking the streets while my son lies in a grave and Mitch rots in prison? I can't just live with this."

Aunt Katie cried into a towel, then gazed up at Lucas. "Does Mitch think we're in danger? Are those guys watching us?"

Lucas shook his head. "He has no way of knowing, but I'm sure they've let their guards down since Mitch's conviction. Still, we need to be cautious."

After a few moments of silence, Grandma Janie rose to her feet. "I see two options here," she said. "We can stand down, let Mitch carry the cross, and take his secret to our graves. Or we can reap justice for both Gunner and Mitch."

All eyes remained on Grandma.

Momma was in disbelief. "You mean, by killing Lance and Chester?"

Grandma raised her brows. "The idea is definitely appealing right now."

Dad spoke up, "It would be good enough for them."

"Wait a minute," I objected. "Let's think about this. Do we want justice or revenge? Big difference."

Grandma nodded. "Two wrongs don't make a right, I suppose" she looked to Lucas. "We're going to need Mitch's complete cooperation."

"I'll deal with Mitch, but still, proving his innocence will involve a lot of hard work." Lucas said.

"I'm not afraid of work," Grandma said. "Who's with me?"

Aunt Katie threw down her towel, and stood. "I'm not afraid, either. They took my only child and I won't have him die in vain."

My Momma choked back tears. She took Dad's hand and they stood together. Lucas and I also rose. Uncle Stan placed both hands on the table and eased himself up. He nodded to Grandma. "It's unanimous, then," he said. "Looks like they done messed with the wrong bunch."

Grandma smiled. "*Osda*. We've got each other's backs. And don't be fretting over me none. I keep a loaded shotgun next to the bed."

"Okay," Lucas said. "Let's get this ball rolling."

Grandma looked around the table, her face beamed with pride. "Keepers. This is just how I raised you. Now you understand why we take care of our own. We'll make them pay for what they did to our family. Like the old saying goes, the chickens always come home to roost."

A few days later, Lucas visited with Mitch again. He told him about the family meeting. Mitch didn't want to get us involved. "This is not what I intended," he said.

Lucas didn't budge. "I need everything you've got, Mitch."

Mitch shook his head. "Don't you see? Chester will kill you all. I can't live it."

"Grandma said to tell you, like it or not this is how it is. She's expecting information when I get home, and I'm not leaving here empty-handed."

Mitch slid his hands up and down his thighs, nervous. "No, I won't do this."

"I warned them of the risks," Lucas told him.

"Warned them? You should be helping me to protect them."

"Like I said, this is how it's going to be."

Mitch shook his head. "The decision is mine."

"Would you shut the hell up and listen to me? I'm not leaving without getting what I came for."

"You goddamned hard heads." Mitch snapped. He held his face in his hands for a few moments. "I should have known this would happen. Where do you want me to start?"

Our next family meeting was Friday night, at the farm. Mom and Aunt Katie served a fried chicken supper with all the trimmings. My Dad came through the door a little late, and apologized for having to work over-time. He shook hands with Lucas and Uncle Stan before planting a kiss on mom's forehead.

"We started without you, James." Grandma teased.

Dad grinned. "That's quite alright, Janie. I've been looking forward to this meal all day."

She passed a basket of biscuits.

Dad patted her hand. "Still spoiling me, are you?"

"With pleasure."

After supper, we sipped our iced tea, as Lucas told us the latest information from Mitch. Though Gunner hired Mitch for a security position at The Foxhole, Chester kept increasing his duties. Chester worked directly under Lance, and was only supposed to hang around until Gunner had the place up and running.

Chester always had weed and crystal meth on him. Mitch found this out after he complained about a long day's work at the mill. "This will pep you right up," Chester said, and gave Mitch some product to try.

The following weekend, Mitch asked for more, but offered to pay this time. Chester wouldn't take any money. "I got you covered," he said. Mitch asked him not to say anything to Gunner.

Chester often invited Mitch to sit outside with him and talk. Chester knew how to sell, as he easily struck up conversations with customers in the parking lot. It didn't take long for Mitch to catch on. One night, Chester told Mitch he had to be somewhere, and asked him to try his hand at selling. Chester gave Mitch a zippered bag with content inside, and promised to make it worth his while. At that point, Mitch was using more frequently, and he agreed.

Mitch soon realized that selling drugs was just as vital to The Foxhole as beer was. But why tell Gunner? Mitch felt the two operations could run separately, and never considered one interfering with the other. He also kidded himself about his own use, thinking he could take it or leave it. But he started using every day. Valerie heard rumors, and then she saw his behavior begin to change. She had no idea who Mitch's source was.

Eventually, she spoke to Gunner, and told him of her suspicions. When Gunner confronted Mitch, he eventually owned up to it. To get Gunner off his back, he promised to stop. Fortunately for Mitch, Gunner only knew he was using, he didn't know Mitch was selling, too.

Soon after, Chester handed off all the sales to Mitch. The pay was good, but Mitch snorted most of it up his nose. Chester told him to confine the deals to the parking area, and to keep Gunner out of it, no deals inside the bar.

Mitch started selling everywhere: at the local gas station, the mill, even his own front porch. One night, a knock on the door woke Valerie up; it was some stranger looking to buy drugs. That's when she realized what was going on right under her nose. She went to Gunner, who in turn met with Mitch, told him what he knew, and threatened to fire him.

Mitch panicked. He needed the bar job to sustain his habit. He asked Chester for help, and Chester told him not to worry, and to leave things up to him. Chester talked Gunner into giving Mitch a second chance. But Mitch's habit grew substantially, as did his debt to Chester. Their arguments became increasingly violent.

After Valerie packed up and left, Mitch's life went into a nosedive. Since things had soured with Chester, Mitch feared he'd assign the sales to someone else.

Gunner was rarely speaking to Mitch, and when he did, it was ugly. Soon, Chester realized what he'd created, and had no choice but bring Lance into the situation. During a meeting with Chester and Mitch, Lance questioned Chester's worries. "Why can't you guys get along? Mitch is making us money, right? Give him more responsibilities to pay off his debt. I expect you both to get your issues worked out."

But Chester wanted Mitch out of the operation, so he fabricated a story to discredit him, and convinced Lance that Mitch had sold to a cop's teenaged son. Mitch vehemently denied it.

My Dad and Uncle Stan listened in silence, but I could see the wheels turning. When Lucas finished, Uncle Stan spoke up. "Alright, now that we have the background, we need to bring ourselves current on Lance and Chester. What they look like, where they live, what they drive, who they run with, their daily routines.

"How do we find that all out?" Aunt Katie wondered. "They live in Arkansas, and you both work full time jobs."

"I'll hire a private detective," Stan said, "and it'll be worth every red cent. For the time being, though, we should all be alert. Do your errands together, ladies, and try not to venture out alone."

Dad joined in. "Yes, security is the priority, and we need to be prepared to protect ourselves. If we get the case re-opened, Lance and Chester are going to hear about it."

Grandma nodded. "My gun is locked and loaded, as Gunner used to say. I reckon that's all I need."

Mom wasn't so sure. "You live alone, Mother, which could make you an easy target. Maybe you'll consider staying with James and me a while?"

Grandma Janie interrupted her. "I'll be fine. And you're just a phone call away." Grandma rose to retrieve a pie from the oven. Momma rolled her eyes and sighed in defeat.

"What's next?" Lucas asked.

Aunt Katie answered matter-of-factly. "We'll bring Mitch's story to the district attorney and pray that he'll support us."

Grandma Janie peered over her shoulder, then turned to face us, hands on her hips. "Alright everyone, let's close this meeting. It's time for pie and ice cream."

Our family started making deposits into Mitch's prison account. He used some of the money for greeting cards and writing supplies, so he could send us mail. Grandma's face lit up with every letter that she found in her mailbox.

Sometime mid-Summer, Mom called me at work to say that she and Aunt Katie had rushed Grandma to the emergency room with a high fever. She was diagnosed with a urinary tract infection, given iv fluids and released. "She's agreed to stay with me and your dad tonight." Mom said.

"Good," I replied. "She needs to rest. Let me and Lucas know if we can help."

After hanging up, I went back to work, riddled with worry over Grandma's health. Her grief for Uncle Ted and Gunner had obviously worn her down. Not to mention her concerns for Mitch. I felt that time could be growing short. Our mission for justice would need to be swift and aggressive.

Two weeks later, we managed to get an appointment with District Attorney, Dillon "Bulldog" Harper. We seated ourselves before his massive oak desk. Harper was thick chested with large jowls, much like a bulldog. Known for being sharp and relentless, he had earned a lot of respect in our county. He remained quiet while Lucas and Uncle Stan laid out the scenario. He looked over the statements, and studied the documentation from the PI. When he finished, he stood and gazed out the window at the courtyard below. After a moment, he turned to face us.

"I have to admit, your case is well-built. It's very believable, and you have obviously done your homework. That aside, I just want to make you aware of how difficult it is to overturn a conviction. In essence, I'm saying that it's very rare. Assuming the previous investigation was incompetent, this case could leave a nasty smear on the face of the sheriff's department. For which reason, they may not be terribly cooperative."

"Mitch pled guilty," I said. "I don't see how anything could hurt the sheriff's reputation."

"Well, officers tend to be sensitive about these things."

Grandma didn't bat an eye. "What do you suggest we do?" she asked.

Bulldog folded his arms across his chest. "Mrs. Samuels, I really hope you've considered…"

She interrupted. "You're saying you won't help us?"

He held up a forefinger. "I don't believe you understand the magnitude of your request. If you like, maybe I can explain it in greater detail?"

Grandma stood abruptly. "We'll take a yes or a no. Maybe's don't count."

Bulldog looked at the floor and chuckled, which was not a good move. Grandma lifted her purse, and bustled from his office, the rest of us close behind her. Bulldog followed, then called down the hall after us. But we were already loading onto the elevator. It'd been a long time since I had seen Grandma walk so fast. She definitely had a fire inside her that day. "On to Plan B," she told us. "I have an idea."

A few days later, I received a call from Grandma Janie, asking if I would drive her for an errand the following day. She also asked that I keep the errand to myself for the time being. I agreed, and saved my questions for later.

I kissed Lucas goodbye the next morning, and drove to the farm. Grandma was waiting, purse on her arm. I helped her down the porch steps and into the Jeep. I slid behind the wheel and paused. "Okay, where are we going?"

I have an appointment with the sheriff," she said.

We made small talk during the drive. But with my imagination going wild, my nerves were in a bundle and my stomach felt weak. Whatever her plan was, Grandma wasn't sharing. Hopefully this meeting would go better than the last one.

I took her to the station, then went around to help her out. But when I reached to take her arm in mine, she gently pulled away. "I'm doing this by myself. You can stay out here. Go have something to nibble on while I'm gone. You look pale."

I looked at her, puzzled.

"I won't be long," she said. "But if I am, bring bail money." She winked and walked away.

I watched until she was out of sight, then went to a nearby coffee shop. I took a seat by the window and tried to drink my coffee, but couldn't shake the sick feeling inside. Was something about to happen?

Thirty-five minutes later, Grandma reappeared. I hurried to her side and asked if everything went okay. She just nodded and got into the Jeep. Once we were on our way back, she told me what happened.

"I sat in front of Sheriff Calhoun," she said. "who had that usual smirk on his face. I've never liked him. He asked what he could do for me, and I told him point-blank, 'I need you to re-open my grandson's case.' He balked at the thought of it. I told him Mitch's story, same as we told the DA last week. But I could tell he didn't believe a word I was saying.

"He kept cutting me off with, 'Mitch pled guilty.'" I said, 'I don't care what Mitch pled at the time, Sheriff. He was strung out on drugs, and not to mention, traumatized. And to make matters worse, Mitch was threatened and scared. He did what he had to do in order to save his family. Wouldn't you do the same?''

"He finally looked at me like I was a real human being. 'Well, Mrs. Samuels, I see your point, but I also believe I might say just about anything to get myself out of prison.'"

"I assured him that wasn't the case, as Mitch was extremely reluctant to offer his cooperation in the first place. But Sheriff Calhoun still wasn't convinced. 'What makes you so certain Mitch is telling the truth?' he asked. 'We gave him every opportunity to come clean, and so did his public defender.' I tried to drive it into the sheriff's thick skull that Mitch's plea was to protect us, and that he truly believed he caused Gunner's death. Though his addiction did contribute, it didn't actually pull the trigger of that gun.

"His voice softened then. 'It's not that I don't trust your opinion,' he told me. 'After all, you're a well-respected citizen and you obviously love your grandchildren. But without solid evidence…'"

"We have evidence, I explained, but we need your cooperation, and a good detective. One who isn't prejudiced, maybe. He frowned like I had spit on him. 'What's that supposed to mean?' he asked.

"I enlightened him that since he had taken office, I'd heard of plenty injustices from my Cherokee community. I also reminded him about an incident back in his high school days, after my Katie came home crying. When I asked her what was wrong, she told me that Jerry Calhoun had tried to force a kiss on her, and when she pushed him away, he called her a dirty half-breed. I could see the wheels spinning in his head. That's when I went in for the kill. 'Be a real shame if that got out now, just before election. Too many good men's careers have ended over foolish things said long ago.' Then I stood up and demanded he do the right thing, and re-open the case of an innocent man who sits in prison.

I was almost speechless with her show of courage and determination. I was so proud; I could feel my eyes welling up. I parked outside her house and just sat there for a few moments, completely in awe. "What do you think he'll do, Grandma?"

She opened the vehicle door. "Well, I believe he'll consider my request, probably only because he is up for re-election. But as Benjamin Franklin once said, 'A spoonful of honey will catch more flies than a gallon of vinegar.' So, I sweetened the pot just a tad. I promised that if he gave our case a fair and thorough investigation, he'd have my outspoken support come election time. Considering that thirty percent of our county's population is Native American, I believe he got my message."

She looked deep into my eyes. "By the way, when are you going to buy a nice car? This Jeep is too tall, and the ride is very uncomfortable. You should be driving a family vehicle now."

I blinked a couple of times before offering a defense. "Well, I really like my Jeep. What's the rush to get a family vehicle?"

She patted my shoulder. "Because you're with child. Go ahead and have your doctor confirm it, but I'm never wrong about these things."

Within two days, Grandma received a call from Sheriff Calhoun. Mitch's case was officially re-opened, with a detective already assigned. Grandma told us he was coming to her place at five p.m. the next day, and invited us all out to meet him.

The next day, everyone showed up early. Grandma wore a brightly colored apron over her clothing, with earrings to match. She puttered around, straightened cups and saucers, and made sure the cream and sugar dishes were full.

"Looks like we're all here," I informed her.

At quarter to five, everyone sat down at the kitchen table. "Are y'all ready for this?" Uncle Stan asked.

We all nodded. Aunt Katie patted Grandma's arm. "Momma, I don't know what you said to Jerry Calhoun, but you certainly lit a fire under his ass."

There was a rap on the front door.

Lucas stood. "I'll get it."

He came back with the detective, a Native American man. He looked to be in his thirties, and very handsome. He sat his brown leather briefcase down and scanned the room.

Lucas introduced him. "This is Detective Sam Little Bear. I'll let you introduce yourselves."

With introductions aside, Mr. Little Bear retrieved an ink pen and a legal pad from his briefcase. Though soft-spoken, his tone was confident. "Thank you all for having me over tonight, and please, call me Sam. I look forward to getting to know you all, but first I'll tell you a few things about myself. I'm originally from Pushmataha County. I was born and raised there and served under the sheriff for ten years. I have always liked it here in Chero-kee County, though. So, when an opening came up, I ap-plied for it and decided to move. That was almost a year ago, and so far, so good."

He kept looking around as he spoke, then he walked to a window and gazed out at the backyard. "Excuse me, folks," he said. "I keep getting a feeling I've been here before."

Grandma spoke. "That's because you have."

We all stared at her, wide-eyed.

"I'm a friend of your Grandma Delores. She brought you here a couple of times when you were very young."

He gasped. "It's beginning to come back to me, Mrs. Samuels. I was very close to my grandmother, and I miss her." He pointed to the garden out back. "You took us out there, didn't you?"

She nodded. After that, Sam took his seat and addressed us one by one. He made notes and asked a lot of questions about Gunner's relationship with Mitch. An hour later, we broke for coffee. Uncle Stan went to the front porch to smoke a cigarette. Sam followed him out.

"The longer I'm here," Sam Little Bear said, "the more familiar things are becoming." He pointed to the corner of Grandma's yard. "Didn't a tire swing used to hang from that tree?"

"Yeah," Stan said. "A storm came through and blew the limb down."

Sam smiled. "I remember playing on it."

"Most kids around these parts played on it, at one time or another," Stan told him. "I guess I should have hung it back up. Just never got around to it. You know how time flies. Next thing I knew, my son…" Uncle Stan hesitated, then swallowed his emotions. "Gunner was in Vietnam."

"I know this is difficult. Many things are going to be brought back up. I just want to prepare you and Mrs. Lane."

Uncle Stan shook his head. "It's okay. Seems like we've re-lived Gunner's death every damned day. We know this won't bring him back, but my wife and I want those killers put away. We're willing to cooperate, one hundred percent. Anything you need."

Back at the table, Sam talked to Grandma last. After a series of questions similar to those he'd asked the rest of us, he laid down his pen and folded his hands together. "I remember coming to Waya to spend Thanksgivings with my grandma."

"You did," Grandma confirmed.

Sam looked around the room, then back to Grandma.

"When you took us to your garden, we picked turnips and greens…And I remember pumpkins."

Grandma smiled warmly.

Sam continued. "You gave us two of them, as a matter of fact. Grandma made a pie with one, and I carved the other into my very first Jack-o'-lantern. It didn't matter that Halloween had passed already; I was happy all the same."

Grandma Janie laughed; her eyes glistened.

Sam Little Bear looked around the table. "My Grandmother's Social Security check didn't always last the entire month. If she was running low on groceries, she always knew who to turn to." He winked at Grandma Janie. "We took the vegetables home, and on Thanksgiving, we had food to eat. There was no turkey, nothing fancy, but still a good nutritious meal. We even roasted the pumpkin seeds to snack on."

Though I had always been proud of Grandma Janie, never so much as in that moment. She blinked through her tears. "Delores was a fine lady and a true friend."

Sam chuckled as another memory came forth, his eyes large with excitement. "And another time, I remember you served us the most delicious pie."

"Dutch apple pie," she said.

Momma spoke up. "Oh, those are the best. She still makes them on occasion."

Everyone at the table nodded in agreement.

When the meeting was over, Sam packed up his briefcase. "I've made arrangements to visit with Mitch. After that, we'll all come together again. You'll be kept completely in the loop throughout this investigation." He turned to Grandma Janie and took her hand. "It's time for me to go to work. I give you my word, this case has my utmost attention."

A few days later, I left the pharmacy early in order to beat Lucas home from work. I'd gone to my doctor that morning, and he confirmed my pregnancy. He also estimated my delivery to be in the spring of 1979. After the news sank it, I felt excited, but scared. I hurried home to make my husband a nice supper of meatloaf, green beans, mashed potatoes, and gravy. Biscuits, too. Lucas had always loved my mother's meatloaf, and I was determined to make mine as delicious as hers.

When he walked in the front door, hot and dusty from work, I handed him a tall glass of iced tea.

He took a large gulp. "Damn, it smells great in here. Why are you home so early?"

I gave him a peck on the lips. "Oh, it was slow at the pharmacy, so I decided to come home and cook you a meatloaf."

"I could get used to this. Let me get a shower. Don't start without me," he teased.

It was perfect timing, as I had just put everything on the dining table when Lucas came back to the kitchen. He wore jeans only, his hair loose and damp. It was thick and beautiful, and longer than mine. During supper, we talked about the good impression Sam Little Bear left on everyone, and how we looked forward to the next meeting.

Lucas spoke between forkfuls. "I believe we're fortunate to have him on the case. I've asked around a little, and he seems to be a solid guy. His reputation is pretty clean."

"Like your plate?" I asked.

He nodded. "This meatloaf was your best yet. Thank you." He picked up his plate and carried it to the sink.

I stood and walked up behind him. "So, my cooking has improved, eh?"

He turned and placed both hands on my shoulders. "Absolutely. You'll be right up there with both of our momma's very soon." He kissed my lips. "I'm not judging, though. I'd be happy with a bologna sandwich, as long as I'm eating it with you."

He definitely had a way with words. I took his hand. "How about a walk? Let's grab some carrots for Lady and Spirit."

The sun was beginning to drop, and the field was turning gold. The Appaloosas weren't far away, and they came right over.

Lucas checked them over, making sure their health was up to his standards. "God, the memories that start flooding back…These two are like family members."

"Yes." I agreed. "I remember being a little upset when Uncle Ted sold them, but I guess it was for the best."

Lucas continued to dote over them. "I can't wait to get a few of my own."

My perfect opportunity. "A few?" I said, "Horses or children?"

He looked at me. "Come to think of it, both."

I gazed into his dark eyes. "Can you wait until spring?"

His face lit up. "You're buying me a horse?"

"No," I laughed. "But I'll give you a child. How's that?"

His mouth fell open. "Sara? Ser—Seriously?" he stammered. He scooped me up and whirled me around in a circle. The Appaloosas picked up on our excitement, and playfully pawed at the ground.

Lucas put me down and placed a hand on my stomach. "Have you been sick?"

I shook my head. "Very little, actually. I had no idea until Grandma Janie told me."

"She diagnosed you? I'm not surprised."

After telling Lady and Spirit goodnight, we went back inside. We were anxious to spread the news, but decided to wait until the weekend.

"Let's tell them in person." Lucas suggested. His face was stuck in a smile for the rest of the evening.

The first week of October, 1978 was rainy and cold. Grandma Janie called early, to tell us about our next meeting with Sam Little Bear. "Be here tomorrow at five a.m.," she said.

"Five a.m., on Saturday morning?" I asked. "Are you for real?"

"Yes, granddaughter. The protection ceremony must take place at first light, so dress warm."

Though she'd occasionally performed these on family members, I'd never witnessed an actual ceremony. "Okay, I understand. We'll be there." I promised.

"We'll make a nice breakfast afterward," Grandma said. "I'm sure *"usdi"* will enjoy it."

"Yes, usdi will, as well as his or her daddy." I winked at Lucas, who was standing beside me.

The following morning, Lucas and I arrived at the farm twenty minutes early. Mom and Dad were already there, along with Uncle Stan and Aunt Katie. Eight lawn chairs sat in a row on one side of Grandma's yard, all facing east.

Everyone gathered outside just before Sam arrived. He was dressed casually; sneakers, jeans, and an OU Sooners sweatshirt.

Grandma instructed us to sit. She pulled a roll of dried tobacco leaves from her coat pocket. Holding the bundle in her left hand, she lifted it towards the overcast sky.

Grandma said a prayer in Cherokee, then reached for an old wooden bowl sitting on her chair. She placed the tobacco inside the bowl, and lit the leaves on fire with a match. Then she blew softly on the embers until the flames died down. Faint smoke drifted from the bowl. Grandma took an eagle feather from her right pocket, and walked to Sam, who sat at the end of the row. She held the bowl high, and used the feather to waft smoke around him, chanting all the while in Cherokee.

She moved down the line, wafting smoke over each of us. When she reached me, at the end of the row, she gave special directions. "Cover your nose and mouth with your coat sleeve."

She repeated the prayer a total of four times throughout the ceremony. Four, she reminded us, was a sacred number. Grandma concluded the ceremony with a short prayer in English. *"Great Creator, we pray that you place your protection upon us…"*

When the ceremony was over, we moved to the kitchen. I helped Mom and Aunt Katie cook breakfast. Grandma supervised and paced between stove and table, pouring coffee and placing silverware.

Sam looked down to admire his plate of over-easy eggs, bacon, and biscuits with gravy. "This is a rare treat for me. It's been a while since I've had homemade gravy and biscuits."

"Do you cook for yourself, or is there a Mrs.?" Grandma asked.

"Actually, I'm divorced." Sam answered. "She left me a couple of years ago…For a white guy."

Everyone looked up at once. At first, we didn't know how to respond, until Uncle Stan burst into laughter. Sam immediately joined in, followed by the rest of us.

"Win some, lose some." Grandma quipped.

"Exactly." Sam agreed. "Well, the other guy had a thicker wallet. I can't say that I blame her. We all know cops don't bring home big paychecks."

"You're definitely not paid your worth," Dad said. With breakfast over, Sam spoke. He started with his prison visit, and told us that Mitch was in good spirits and thoroughly answered every question, from start to finish. "I'm completely convinced that Mitch is telling me the truth." Sam said.

"So, what's next?" Aunt Katie asked.

"I'm going to Arkansas on Monday, hunting for the helicopter pilot. We have an eye witness out there."

We broke into an applause, and he stood to leave. He smiled humbly and waved his hands. "Thank you, but I haven't done that much just yet. I appreciate the delicious breakfast, as well as the prayer of protection." He nodded at Grandma, then pulled two photos from his briefcase and placed them on the middle of the table. "I'd like to leave you with these pictures of Lance Ferguson and Chester Owens. An informant told me that Chester still comes around to check on business at The Foxhole. He drives a newer model white Ford pickup. I'm not sure if the general public knows what we're doing, but I certainly hope

Chester doesn't catch wind that we've re-opened the case. Please stay alert."

After Sam left, we passed around the photos. Seeing the image of Lance's face again made me sick to my stomach. Lucas appeared uneasy, no doubt he was twice as worried for the safety of me and our unborn child.

I caught distinct stares from both mom and Aunt Katie. I could tell that Lucas noticed, too. He shot a sly grin at me from across the table. It was time to let the cat out of the bag for the unsuspecting.

I was about to stand when Aunt Katie blurted out, "Momma, why did you ask Sara to cover her nose during the ceremony?"

My mother touched my arm. "Honey, are you coming down with something?"

Grandma smiled, but stayed mum.

I stood. "Yes, actually, I'm coming down with a baby."

I looked across the table at my parents. "Congratulations, you have a grandchild on the way."

Aunt Katie hugged Momma, and suddenly everyone was crying, myself included. My parents hugged me and Lucas. Uncle Stan thanked us for the wonderful news. "Perfect timing," he said. "This is exactly what our family needed."

Sam started his investigation, and made great progress within the first few weeks. Apparently, there were only a handful of licensed helicopter pilots in the Hot Springs area, so he gathered up the names and tried to track them all down. He reported to us that he'd narrowed the list to three men, and planned to question each of them right away.

Lucas kept up his visits with Mitch, and soon noticed a growing maturity. Mitch had plenty of time on his hands; enough to contemplate his mistakes, to rediscover the value of life and the significance of a healthy body and mind. During their visits, Mitch spoke highly of Sam Little Bear, saying that he already considered him a friend. Though Lucas was impressed with Mitch's progress, he still worried that the guilt on Mitch's shoulders might never go away.

Mitch's correspondence with the rest of our family had been short, sweet, and guarded, but most importantly, he was making headway. He even sent me a congratulations card, and wrote that he was happy for Lucas and me.

Lucas and I made plans to prepare our nursery. We also set a goal of opening the horse training business a few months after our baby's birth. Lucas was ready to leave the construction field and dedicate himself to a new career. We prayed that everything would fall into place.

It was mid-November when Sam called to schedule our next family meeting at Grandma's farm. Us ladies planned a supper for that Sunday afternoon: a pot roast with potatoes and carrots, okra, squash, and yeast rolls. For dessert, Aunt Katie promised to make a true Southern gem, the hummingbird cake. She'd perfected her recipe over the years; a batter so rich and moist, it smelled as beautiful as it looked. The cake had fresh bananas and pineapple, the earthy scents of cinnamon and nutmeg, and a luscious cream cheese frosting. My mouth watered just thinking about it.

At the meeting, we learned that Sam had tracked down the three remaining pilots on his list, and pin-pointed Jeremiah D. Truman as the eyewitness to Gunner's murder. When confronted, Jeremiah was caught completely off-guard. He denied knowing Lance or Chester. He couldn't produce an alibi for the night in question, but claimed that he was nowhere close to Oklahoma.

"I had already done my homework," Sam told us. "and knew his background. Jeremiah was raised in a devout household, the son of a Baptist pastor up in Little Rock. He learned to fly in the Army, and served in Vietnam. It's not clear whether he met Lance there, but there's a good chance. Jeremiah currently works in the lumber industry, flying for timber inspections."

"Does he have a family?" Lucas asked.

"A wife and two young kids. He's also a member of the local Shriners Temple. I'd say he has a lot on the line. Hopefully, he'll weigh out his options and decide to cut a deal for immunity."

Grandma spoke up. "Did he give you the impression he might?"

Sam shook his head. "I'm not so sure, Janie. I left him with my business card and the scripture John 8:32 written on the back."

She smiled. "Then you will know the truth, and the truth will set you free."

Sam continued. "I told him an innocent young man is wasting away behind bars, with a family on the outside hoping to get him back."

Two weeks later, Grandma rose at five a.m. on a frosty December morning. She pulled on her robe and slippers, then went to the kitchen to put on a pot of coffee. As usual, she gazed out the window on her front door. She saw a pickup driving slowly down the road beside her property. It was still dark out, but she could see well enough to know the truck was white. She watched until it disappeared.

A few minutes later, the truck came back from the other way. She stayed on the look-out for the next fifteen minutes, but saw nothing. She started to feel paranoid and silly, and was about to get on with her day when a sudden movement caught her eye from across the field. Someone dressed in camouflage, sneaking across her land.

Grandma picked up the phone and dialed Stan and Katie's home. When Katie answered, Grandma spoke fast and low. "Send Stan up here. There's a man wearing camouflage on the southwest side of my land. He's making his way toward my house. I have to go now."

Grandma hung up the phone just as the intruder neared her yard fence. He angled to one side, and she lost sight of him. The sheriff's office was a good fifteen miles away, so whatever happened next was up to her.

Grandma stepped backward to look down the hallway, and saw his form dart past a window. He was heading for the front of the house. She stayed perfectly still, listening. A moment later, she heard footsteps on the porch.

She dashed to the back door, and listened again. When she heard the old front door knob squeak, she picked up her shotgun and slipped outside. The sky was just beginning to grow lighter. Grandma Janie made use of skills she hadn't used in decades, stalking quietly around the old smoke house. She heard a sudden crash; most likely the front door being kicked in.

Grandma crept to the side of the front porch. She crouched down and listened as he rushed through the house. By the sound of it, he seemed to be searching every room. Once he realized the house was empty, he'd be coming back out. Grandma stood and took her place facing the front door. She dug in her heels and waited for the trespasser. Just as he stepped outside, she racked her shotgun, because there's no sound in the world quite like that.

Chester Owens halted; eyes wide.

Grandma aimed the gun at his chest. "Lookin' for someone?"

He said nothing.

"Put your hands up, nice and slow. And if you think I won't shoot, you're as dumb as you look."

Chester raised his hands, as directed, while she continued to hold him at gunpoint. Within moments, Grandma noticed Stan as he closed in from behind her captive.

Chester shook his head. "You might have me right now, old woman, but it don't matter. We'll get you one way or another."

"Oh yeah? Who's we?" asked a voice from behind Chester. Uncle Stan appeared, holding his .30-30 Winchester.

Chester took a deep breath. Stan pushed the barrel firmly into his back, and spoke through gritted teeth. "Are you the sorry piece of shit who murdered my son?"

Chester didn't comment on that.

Grandma and Stan held him at gunpoint until Little Bear's pickup came tearing down Blackberry Lane. Sam rushed into the yard, gun in hand. He patted Chester down and found a hand gun stuffed down the back of his pants. He then handcuffed him and sat him on the ground. "Looks like your plan backfired, Chester," he said. "I'm going to love taking you to jail. With what you've put this family through, I'd say you're lucky to still have a pulse."

Chester was booked for trespassing and breaking and entering with intent to injure, but despite hours of questioning, he didn't offer an ounce of cooperation. Sam decided to move forward quickly. The following morning, he took to the road, heading for the Oklahoma – Arkansas border.

Jeremiah Truman had just arrived at work, and was crossing the parking lot when Sam stepped into his path. Sam watched as Jeremiah's face drained of expression. Jeremiah glanced over his shoulder to see if his co-workers were watching. "What the hell do you want now?" he demanded.

Sam laughed, hoping to gain the attention of everyone within earshot. "Calm down. I didn't come to arrest you yet. Just wanted to keep you in the loop. Chester Owens has been taken into custody in Cherokee County, Oklahoma. He broke in on a member of Mitch Kincaid's family with a gun, intending to harm her. He's being questioned as we speak. The reason I'm here is simple. I'm giving you one more opportunity to come forth with a statement."

Jeremiah gazed at the ground. "Like I told you before, I wasn't there."

"If any member of that family is threatened or harmed, you're responsible, as far as I'm concerned. It'll be just a matter of time before I lock Lance up, too." Sam said, then threw in a tactfully placed bluff. "Oh, and don't even think about leaving town." Sam turned away. "Sleep on it tonight," he said. "I'll be expecting your call."

The two days after Chester's arrest seemed more like two weeks. My family and I were on pins and needles, not knowing what to expect, if anything. We were always looking over our shoulders, just in case Lance Ferguson chose to follow through on his threat. Aunt Katie was a bundle of nerves and could barely sleep, waiting for the phone to ring with news. I tried extra hard to be cautious, but I wasn't exactly scared. I found sanctuary in Lucas' arms, my warm and peaceful refuge. He'd led me through the dark days since Gunner's death, and I cherished him. I knew he would protect me until his last breath.

I'll never forget the evening that I came home from work to find Lucas standing on the front porch. He jumped off the top step and bolted over to open my door. I got out and hugged him. "What's up, baby?"

He grinned from ear to ear. "Sam called a family meeting for tomorrow."

My heart raced. "Do you think this is it?"

"I hope so. The meeting is set for six p.m. at the farm."

Sam Little Bear looked distinguished in a navy blue suit. His black hair was fresh-cut, and shorter than usual. He sat his briefcase down, but didn't open it right away. "Thanks for coming together on such short notice. There have been a couple of developments, and I wanted to share them with you right away. I visited Mitch earlier, and caught him up on things too. We've interrogated Chester relentlessly, but he absolutely won't budge. Yesterday morning, as he was about to bond out, I got a call from Jeremiah Truman. Several hours later, I met him at the Hot Springs Police Department."

I took Lucas's hand in mine. It's like we were all holding our breaths until Sam's next sentence. You could have hard a pin drop.

"Jeremiah gave his account of what happened the night of Gunner's murder. And his story completely corroborates Mitch's."

Smiles filled the room. Uncle Stan pulled Aunt Katie in for a big hug. Happy tears rolled down my grandmother's cheeks as she whispered. "Thank you, Jesus."

We turned our attention back to Sam.

"I relayed the news to Sheriff Calhoun. He went before the DA, who moved to deny Chester's bail. This morning, Lance Ferguson was picked up for questioning."

"What happens next?" my dad asked.

"I'm confident Jeremiah will be issued immunity for his eyewitness testimony. After formal charges are filed against Lance and Chester for murder, money laundering, drug trafficking, and God knows what else, there should be no reason to hold Mitch any longer. Of course, these things do take time, but I'll do everything I can to get him out as soon as possible."

We stood to applaud our hero.

Sam held up both hands. "Thank you. I truly appreciate your confidence in my work. You've shown great support and bravery the whole time."

Grandma nodded proudly. "Looks like those chickens are finally home to roost."

My maternity leave began in mid-May. I felt great, though I sometimes got short of breath after walking for a while. I had received two baby showers; one thrown by Carl and my co-workers, and the other was hosted by

Gillie. Lucas and I were all set. The nursery was complete, my bag was packed and waiting by the front door in anticipation of the big day.

One week before my due date, Lucas came home from work early, then we were off to my OB appointment. He parked our sedan—which we'd traded my Jeep for—and came around to help me out. I put my feet on the ground and stood. A warm sensation rushed down my legs, and I looked to Lucas in a panic. His eyes grew as big as saucers.

"Sara, did you pee your pants or did your water just break? Are you having contractions?" He put a hand on the top of his head and looked around the parking lot for help.

"No, I'm not in pain," I said. "Just an achy back is all. Why don't you go inside and grab a wheelchair? I'll stay right here and wait."

He took a few steps, then turned around. "No, I'm not leaving you here by yourself." He noticed a female patient coming out of the office doors and whistled loudly. "Hey, ma'am! Could you please send a nurse with a wheelchair? My wife is in labor!"

The lady darted back inside. Seconds later, a nurse was pushing an empty wheel chair across the parking lot. I was rushed inside for an examination. The next thing I knew, I was being wheeled to the hospital next door. My parents arrived an hour later. Soon after, Aunt Katie and Grandma joined them in the waiting area. Then Lucas' Mom and Dad, and finally, Gillie.

Lucas was by my side during labor. As nurses came and went from the room, they brought reassuring messages from our family right down the hall. Occasionally, Lucas would take a break and send Momma in to hold my hand and wipe my brow. Uncle Stan showed up with cheeseburgers for everyone except me. Lucas wolfed one down, then returned to me. Unfortunately for him, I could smell the onions on his breath as soon as he came through the labor room door. "Oh my God, I'm going to throw up." I cried.

He covered his mouth and jumped back a step. "Okay, I'll go get some gum. I'm so sorry, baby."

I shrieked. "Just stay away from me!"

My doctor walked in, just in time to play peacemaker.

"Now, now… Everything will be okay." he patted my hand and then pulled up a stool. "Lucas, you're free to go find a mint while I examine her, but don't be too long."

Lucas bolted for the door and disappeared. Ten minutes later, I was wheeled into the delivery room with Lucas trailing behind me.

Soon thereafter, Laramie Gunner Crow made his first appearance, weighing in at seven pounds, ten ounces. He had dark hair, and a shrill cry that melted our hearts. After the doctor placed him on my chest, Lucas and I looked into our son's eyes for the first time. A nurse went to the waiting room door and announced, "It's a boy!" We could hear the applause and whistles.

While on maternity leave, I allowed time for Laramie to bond with Mom, Aunt Katie, and Grandma Janie. They took turns rocking him, changing his diapers, and tending to his every whimper. Grandma's "baby brave," as she referred to him, seemed to enjoy the attention. Grandma tittered as she brushed his hair. "Look, it's almost long enough to braid," she said.

It had been a while since I'd seen so many smiles in our family. Lucas and I hadn't exactly planned the pregnancy, but Laramie was definitely a Godsend. I loved the moments when Lucas held him, and shared their big plans. "I have so much to teach you, son. We'll start with riding a horse. Then, you'll learn our sacred dances. And little league after that. Once you're older, there'll be hunting and fishing. Oh, and you must learn the Cherokee language, too. But, if you're not into all of this stuff, just tell me. I only want you to be happy."

When Laramie was three months old, my parents offered to babysit while Lucas and I went on a long-awaited date. We drove to Tulsa and met up with Gillie and Jay Bob for dinner and dancing. Lucas and I welcomed a night out on the town, and a chance to hold one another on the dimly lit dancefloor.

Later, after telling our friends goodnight, we drove back to Waya. Passing The Foxhole, it suddenly seemed very strange. For the last few years, it had been a hot spot for the community, with flashing neon lights, rambunctious laughter, and loud thumping music. With Lance

Ferguson now in jail, its doors had closed, and it sat in the shadows, with not a soul in sight.

"Pull over." I ordered.

Lucas slid to a stop on the shoulder. "What's wrong? Are you sick?"

I shook my head. "Do you remember when you said you'd like to see "The Foxhole" burn to the ground?"

"Yeah..."

We turned to look at the darkened building.

Lucas laughed. "You're kidding…Right?"

He put the pickup back in gear. I placed my hand on top of his. Lucas was silent for a moment. "You're serious…"

We drove up to Cemetery Hill and parked close to Gunner's grave. Lucas pulled on his work gloves and took a gas can from the pickup bed. I wanted to go with him, but he wouldn't let me. "I got it. You stay here by Gunner. I won't be long."

"Be careful." I said, and he disappeared into the night.

I sat on the cold ground and patted Gunner's grave. "It's me, cousin. I'm sorry I haven't been here lately, but so much has happened. Your killers are finally in jail, hopefully forever. Your daddy was right when he said, 'They messed with the wrong bunch.' Life isn't the same without you. I know you'd want me to go on with mine, but not a day goes by that I don't miss your smile, and your voice, and even the occasional scolding..." I blinked back my tears. "Lucas and I have a son, Laramie Gunner, and he's the most beautiful baby I've ever seen. I have another surprise for you. It should be happening any minute now."

I saw the first flickers as Lucas came up the hill. Soon the flames were touching the sky. Lucas reached for my hand, and we watched together.

"Burn, baby, burn," I said. Lucas beamed as I clasped his face in my hands. "You amaze me."

"If that ain't love," he gestured to the blazing horizon, "I don't know what is."

He picked me up and swung me around. We took the backroads home, driving with the headlights off.

While awaiting his release, Mitch worked to repair relationships. He discovered that it was easier to express his feelings through letter writing, and he became quite good at it.

On November 20th, 1979, Lucas rose early and proudly declared that today would mark his last trip "to that dreadful prison." I walked him to the door and offered to ride along. He shook his head. "I don't want to overwhelm Mitch. Let's give him time to settle in at Grandma's house. You'll see him on Thanksgiving." I wanted to insist, but if anyone knew Mitch's state of mind, it was Lucas. I trusted his intuition.

I scooped up a framed photo from the entry table; Gunner, Lucas and Mitch together at Mitch and Valerie's wedding. Though suddenly overcome with sadness, I reminded myself that this was a happy day.

A few weeks earlier, Lucas and I bought Uncle Ted's home, and had been making preparations to open our business, "Crow Hill Equine." Lucas would offer cutting horse training, a technique that teaches horses to herd and separate cattle.

Lucas waited outside the prison for thirty minutes before Mitch stepped through the gates wearing boots, jeans, and a western shirt. They stopped for lunch on the way to Grandma's house, and Lucas told him to order whatever he wanted; which was a BBQ brisket sandwich, potato salad, and a glass of sweet tea. Afterwards, Mitch thanked him for the meal and said, "It was good…But not as good as Grandma's."

Lucas chucked. "Nothing is. Let's get you home."

They made small talk about horses and high school friends on the way. Lucas broached the next subject carefully. "If you're interested, I could use some help from time to time. You seem to be healthy enough to work with horses."

Mitch smiled, "Yeah, I'd like that. I'm sure I can help out." He was quiet for a moment, then said, "I don't think I'd be here today if it weren't for you, Lucas. There were so many times I considered…" He waved his hand, unable to finish.

Lucas glanced at him. "Don't mention it, brother. You got through it and I'm proud of you."

Mitch took a letter from his pocket. "I have to give some credit to Grandma, too. She sent me this scripture a while back. She said it was the same scripture she gave to

Gunner when he left for Vietnam. I guess I've read it about a million times."

"What does it say?" Lucas asked.

"It's from the book of Psalms. "I will lift up mine eyes unto the hills, from whence cometh my help. My help cometh from the Lord, which made heaven and earth. He will not let your foot be moved; he who keeps you will not slumber."

Mitch continued, "I've read the Bible from front to back, probably several times while I was locked up. Some of it I understand, some not so much. But this scripture was my refuge."

When they reached Waya, Mitch had a special request. "Do you mind taking me to the cemetery?" he asked. Lucas drove to Cemetery Hill and waited in the pickup. He watched as Mitch knelt by Gunner's grave. He touched the letters etched on the gravestone, Gunner Elias Lane. Then he bowed his head to pray.

They turned onto Blackberry Lane at dusk, and found Grandma waiting from the porch swing. Tears streamed down Mitch's face when he rushed up the front steps to embrace her. After a moment, Grandma stepped back and looked Mitch over. "You're too thin," she said. "But I have a remedy for that." She winked at him, and gestured toward the front door. "Come on in, boys. I have a pecan pie in the oven."

Lucas and I slept late the following morning. We cuddled, and he traced my jawline with his finger. "I drove past that old hotel on the way home last night," he told me.

"You mean "our" hotel, where we made loooove for the first time?" I giggled loudly.

"Ssshhh…You're going to wake Laramie. I was hoping for a chance to re-enact that night."

As I looked into his eyes, my butterflies awakened. "I remember it as if it was yesterday."

Lucas pulled me underneath him, and pushed down a strap of my nightie. Just as he was about to kiss me, I stopped him.

"Not like this," I said.

He squinted and shook his head.

"This isn't how it happened." I sat up and slid off the bed. "As I recall, I came out of the bathroom in my underwear. You were standing with your back to me. And you were shirtless."

I walked toward the bathroom and shot a smoldering look over my shoulder.

He leaned back on his elbows and grinned. "Oh, my Lord, you're so naughty. All right, it's on."

After breakfast, I busied myself cleaning the kitchen. When the phone rang, I yelled to Lucas, "Babe, can you get that? My hands are wet."

After a brief conversation, Lucas laughed and hung up the phone. He filled me in as I finished the dishes. "That was Mitch, telling me about his first day of freedom. "He took his coffee to the front porch. Said the field looked pretty with the frost, and it sparkled like heaven. He got an odd feeling, like he was being watched. He thought it was paranoia from being in prison. Until he heard a snort."

I smiled. "The welcome home gifts?"

Lucas nodded. "Lady and Spirit recognized him from the corner of the corral. He carried his coffee out to see them."

I was excited to hear more. "So, he was surprised?"

"Sure was," Lucas said. "He said thank you, and he plans to start riding them right away."

I dried my hands. "Well, I'm happy Molly agreed to sell them. With their youngest kid in college now, it's only right the horses come back to us."

"He mentioned you," Lucas said.

"What did he say?"

"He wants to see you privately. Tomorrow, before Thanksgiving dinner. He asked if we can come a little early. I said yes. Okay with you?"

Tears filled my eyes. Lucas placed his hand on my shoulder. "I was hoping to make you smile, not cry. Remember, we have so much to be thankful for."

Lucas was absolutely right. Thanksgiving morning was windy and gray. I rose early to cook my dishes for the meal. Afterward, I got dressed and sat down at my vanity to do my makeup and hair. After Lucas loaded the food into his pickup, he came in for me and Laramie. We drove past the stables and onto the paved road.

We kept the conversation casual, which seemed to help my jittery nerves. Laramie babbled from his car seat. We parked in front of the grandma's house, carried Laramie and the food, and climbed up the porch steps.

Grandma's face lit up when she answered the door, and immediately pulled Laramie from his daddy's arms. "There's my boy," she cooed, and whisked him away.

I was about to step inside when Lucas stopped me. He took the food trays from me and nodded toward the field, where Mitch rode Lady by the pond. I rushed to the edge of the porch and waved wildly. Mitch picked up the pace and headed my way.

I hurried out the gate and walked to meet them. Mitch wore a black cowboy hat, much like the one Uncle Ted used to wear. He stopped and dismounted before me. He stalled briefly, and turned his face away. I wasn't sure what to do.

"Don't you start crying," he said.

"You're not the boss of me," I teased.

The tears flowed as I rushed to him. He opened his arms wide and we embraced, unable to speak for a few moments, we waited for the emotions to wash over us. After a few moments, he slid his hands down my arms. "You're even more beautiful than I remember. Life's been good to you, Sara."

As he stood before me, I recognized the Mitch of long ago. Gone was my last image of him, a guilt-ridden addict who stood before the judge.

"Thanks," I said, "Though I have to give some credit to Lucas. He takes excellent care of me. How does it feel to be back after almost three years?"

He looked around at the farm. "Over-whelming at times, like when the memories come flooding back. But I'm home now, where I belong." He leaned against his saddle, "I need to apologize to you. I wish I could make you understand why I shut down like I did."

I shook my head. "It's okay…"

"No, it's not okay," he said. "You stood by me, and believed in me, even after I treated you so badly."

I reached for his arm and we walked together. "The darkness is behind us now. Let's leave it there."

He wiped his eyes and changed the subject. "I can't tell you how much it means to have the horses here. I took Spirit our earlier."

"They're probably just as happy to see you."

"It was nice of you to name Laramie after Gunner. I look forward to meeting him."

I nodded toward the house. "Well, good luck prying him from his Great-Grandmother's arms. It's funny…Though he's the image of his daddy, I sometimes see you and Gunner in him."

We strolled arm in arm, as Lady followed behind us. "Guess who came to the pharmacy the other day?" I asked.

He shrugged.

"Valerie. And she mentioned you."

He seemed intrigued. "Wow, she's still around here?"

"Yes, and she's single."

He eyed me suspiciously. "Are we playing match-maker?"

I winked. "Maybe. When you're ready."

"That's another apology I owe."

I tried to keep his spirits up. "I know it's hard to talk about the past right now, but it'll get easier. Just be patient with yourself."

He smiled. "Grandma taught you well, Sara. Where would I be without you?"

I gripped his arm. "You're strong, and you're just fine with or without me." We hugged again before I turned to go inside.

Mitch led Lady away. "No, I'll always need my keeper."

Inside, the table was set with every piece of china that Grandma owned. There would be no empty places this year. Laramie's booster sat on Uncle Ted's chair, and Gunner's place was reserved for our special guest, Sam Little Bear.

Once we were all present, Dad placed the bronzed turkey on the table. "Okay," Grandma said, "lets join hands now."

Every holiday of my entire life, we'd waited for Grandma to bow and begin the prayer. This time, she hesitated and looked to Mitch, who sat by her side. She lifted his hand and kissed it, then nodded. Mitch, to everyone's surprise, led the prayer that day.

"Dear Lord, as we gather before you, we give thanks for this wonderful meal and the loving hands that prepared it. We ask that you Bless over our friends and loved ones, as we remember those who are no longer with us. Please continue to guide us through the seasons of our lives, from the sunniest of days to the darkest of nights. This we ask in your precious name, Amen."

"Amen." we repeated in unison.

Uncle Stan lifted a basket of dinner rolls. "Let's start with these," he said, and passed them on to Mitch.

Mitch admired the food in front of him. "What a spread. It's like a dream come true."

Momma laughed, as she pushed a spoon into Laramie's open mouth. "Look at him! He loves the mashed potatoes."

"Go easy." Lucas joked. "We're going to my parent's house later and Mom will want a turn."

Aunt Katie shot a stealthy look across the table. "So, Sam…Are you dating anyone?"

Mitch snickered and elbowed Sam. "Uh oh, watch out."

Uncle Stan rolled his eyes.

Sam looked around. "Why? Is this an ambush?"

Mitch nodded toward me. "Matchmaking runs in the female side of the family."

Curiosity was killing me. "Who do you have in mind for him, Aunt Katie?"

She gave me a sly smile. "Oh, I've met a few single ladies down at the beauty shop."

Sam played along. "I'll tell you what, Katie. If you show me one who cooks like you girls do, I'll give her some serious consideration."

Grandma stood up. "Speaking of which…" She pulled a baking dish from the oven, and carefully set the bubbling Dutch Apple pie before Sam. His eyes lit up like a kid on Christmas morning. He reached for her hand. "Thank you, Janie. It smells heavenly. And I'm honored to share this day with you and your family."

She squeezed his hand. "You are family."

As we drove away that evening, I recalled moments of my childhood. Days when all we had was time. Moments such as my cousins and I, chasing chickens and playing under the big oak tree. And of Lucas, dressed in full regalia, dancing across Blackberry Lane.

I watched Grandma Janie in the rear-view mirror, as she stretched the phone cord across the porch to chat with a friend. While Lady and Spirit grazed in the field, somewhere out in the tall grass, Aspen's memory ran free.

After we passed the little church, we happened upon a beautiful tree with branches that stretched high over the road. For whatever reason, I'd never noticed it before. It stood in an autumnal splendor; its golden leaves scattered across the dark asphalt below. As we rolled by, they swirled up, danced with the wind, and settled back to the ground again. Lucas turned up the radio as Fleetwood Mac's Landslide came on.

We traveled past the post office, where the Oklahoma flag rippled in the breeze. Onward, we crossed the iron bridge, and I gazed at the dark river below. The same river which flowed to the crossing; where my cousins had fallen together. Things had come full circle for my family, and the obstacles that had once threatened our future were now behind us.

That night, I opened a bedroom window and settled into Lucas's arms. As the sweet air rushed in, my lullaby began…The song of the fields.

Acknowledgements

To my wonderful family, thank you for your continued love and support:

Torren Valdez, Jarred Valdez, Jackie & Mary Helen Morris, and Rhonda (Morris) Nix.

To the dear friends who've encouraged me to reach for my stars:

Patricia (Youngblood) Kligora, Santana Yturralde, Kimberly Wisch-Lowhorn, Michael Gamerano, and Sara Johnson.

For providing exemplary services and talent, I'm forever grateful to:

John Robert Marlow/The Editorial Department, Rochelle Skorka, Laura Ross Lindly, Jerry D. Bice, Ray S. Smith, and IngramSpark

Last, but definitely not least, I'd like to give thanks to my savior, Jesus Christ.

Sherry Valdez is from Southeastern Oklahoma, where she and her sister were raised on a cattle farm by hard-working, salt of the earth parents. Sherry is the mother of two sons and now resides in Arizona.